This book is dedicated to all those that helped me gather
the stones that helped build the mountain of my life and to
all those that are still gathering their own. Never stop.

I value and
treasure you!

CONTENTS

AN APPEAL

Making an appeal like this does not come naturally to me. I am a first time author. If you were not aware, the algorithm that controls what is and is not displayed, and most importantly, where it is displayed, can be a fickle thing.

I would be honored if you could drop a review. Whether its positive or negative, does not matter. Let your voice be heard. If you loved this book, great. I would love to hear from you. If you hated it, your opinion also greatly matters to me as I embark on this journey.

This applies to any book you read. They each represent the author laying a part of them out, flaying it down to the core, and letting the world gaze upon it. However that makes you feel, let it be known. Every little step helps in making a dream become real.

HONOR

Charles Heuer

PROLOGUE

The Satellite, Gliese 667 C Beta, floated quietly in the deep reaches of the Gliese system. It was of Terran construction, first launched when the humans had been given the system after they joined the Galactic Council via their delivery of Rip Drive technology. Its task was a simple one, to observe.

It was a utilitarian construction. Every sensor imaginable had been meticulously added to its hull and interfaced with the existing computers. On the terminals within the tiny construct, countless displays of information were being gathered and analyzed. It scrolled by the crew in a blaze of numbers and letters. It would be transmitted in its entirety via laser array deeper into Terran space. After that, it would quickly hop aboard the Terran high priority network, a series of arrays that transmitted via a recently perfected use of the quantum entanglement of particles. Finally, it would be delivered straight into the hands of the Terrarch, the matriarch over all of humanity. The first step would be its longest, the final, the most important.

The last time the station had been retrofitted was almost half a century ago when it began tracking its current focus. Since then, there had been a constant presence of Terrans, ensuring that any issues could be addressed and the accuracy of any sensor readings verified. The small crew, four Terrans that had been posted to the satellite for over a year, were gathered, arms wrapped bracingly around each other's shoulders as they gazed at the terminal between them grimly. The most recent calculation of one of the cruisers in the Xen'wa fleet as it slowly approached via sublight rested menacingly on the screen. It was a terrible thing, a cruel machination of fate that would cut their hopes short, a small red X where the cruiser's expected trajectory passed through the silent satellite.

The crew could have hailed the ship, alerted them to their presence. It might have worked to get them through and survive the night's events. The Xen'wa might have shifted their course.

But the crew knew what they would be doing if they broke silence, knew the potential cost of it if the Xen'wa were aware that the Terrans were watching. The crew looked around at one another without a single word marring the silent air between them, understanding. They had already made their choice before the last of the evacuation ships had left several days prior. The crew sent a singular command to the defense AI, one of the greatest treasures that they kept private from the other species and hidden well from view. The defense AI controlled the two hundred and fifty drones that patrolled the system. After which, they all went to wait in their separate ways.

The satellite maintained its silence.

When the Xen'wa cruiser entered into the system, it registered a small collision with a bit of space debris. Such things were of common occurrence and the officer that was at the terminal paid it no mind. Their ships were designed to handle such collisions.

They did not see.

CHAPTER ONE

"It is one thing to see. Anyone can do it. It takes minimal effort to gaze upon the world around you, take its sight in, and go 'Behold!'

A wiser man seeks to understand, to lay bare the truth that lies beneath. Only then can you truly see."

-- Wisdoms of the Terrarch

Boer stared into the mirror, taking in the implanted eye in her left socket. It was motionless, fully dilated, still completely disengaged. The surgery had gone well, but, of course, it should have. They weren't installing anything new, just swapping out for a different model. She raised one hand, tapping out a sequence on her brow, and watched as it started to activate. It took a moment to warm-up and go through the initial boot, but finally, it began moving. She watched as it focused and moved, contracted and widened, bounced jerkily in its berth before slowly syncing up with her natural one. It truly was a remarkable thing, a perfect match for its organic counterpart. The engineers had done a marvelous job in making it undetectable, even if you knew to look for it. It continued its motions, zooming in and out, twitching left and right, before it finally settled. Finally completely synced with her natural eye, it felt so calm and smooth in her body, like it belonged and had always been there. She tapped the final confirmation signal on her brow. Vision in the eye flicked on as it finished establishing itself and started sending signals down her optic nerve, long since treated and modified for this very thing.

She placed a finger in her left ear and worked it violently back and forth. That one continued to let out the occasional hiss, but she knew that this was to be expected with this type of technology. Boer was very well adjusted to these types of implants. She had received her first set when she was little older than seven. While her visual binding had gone off without a hitch, the nerves in her ear had been far more stubborn. She had needed additional surgeries to get it to settle. New implants didn't always join the body quietly, and she was fortunate that it was just her ear that gave issues. She worked her jaw back and forth, trying to help it settle when she heard a loud pop, indicating that it was fully seated and connected. All of the sounds that she could hear out of that ear were now natural once more, no longer filtered through the constant background whine of the mechanics.

Finally silent, she brushed a strand of her long, brown hair out from her face, taking in her simple features. She was by no stretch of imagination a beautiful woman. Boer had no misconceptions about that idea. She looked like she could be anyone. Boer liked that, in a way. The only thing that would ever make her stand out was who she was, not what she was. She smiled to herself before leaning back from the sink and hopping into the shower, letting the water run over her to carry away the last bit of the markings the doctors had scribed over her body.

It had been a quick surgery, in and out. The doctors hadn't even put her under. They just marked her up, gave her a local anesthetic, and then swapped them out. Now that the markings were gone, she wiped her hand through the steamed mirror, taking in her face once more. The surgeons really had done a fantastic job. She doubted that she would have any additional scarring from it. Now clean, dry, and cozy, she set about getting ready for her meeting, working her way through the humble apartment as she dressed herself.

When she had finally finished her preparations, she worked her way to her small desk and sat at the terminal. With a flash of light, the keyboard projected onto the surface before her and she keyed in her new credentials, opening the communication application. She was early enough to have time to sit and think of the weight of it.

She thought of it all, the various small steps she had taken along her way to get here at such a young age and felt it press down upon her, a sense of gravity that, for the briefest of moments, threatened to crush her. She closed her eyes, brought in a deep breath and steadied. She could do this. With a few deft motions, she joined the meeting. On the screen, she could see that three other connections had already been established, the important parties beginning to gather. It was a video conference, an exorbitantly expensive option given the extreme distances of some of those attending.

First was Defense Fleet Admiral Fletcher, a middle-aged man hailing from North America. He was dressed in the sharp fitting dark blues of the defense fleet, uniform set to perfection. He looked into the display from a small conference room, a table stretching before him. Beside him stood a woman of similar age, dressed in the trappings of her position, Vice-Admiral Coeur, his second in command, hailing from Europe. The walls had a metallic sense to them.

He was aboard his ship.

The barest of wrinkles had started to set in around their eyes, a testament to the burden that they had carried over the past sixty years. Only a few strands of his sleek black hair had turned white, providing an accent over the right side of his head. They were both still in their prime by modern standards, still barely touched by age. Coeur's hair had a peppering of gray in it, the strands tightly drawn to the back of her head where it was bundled into a bun. If they so chose, they could only be at the midpoint of their careers. They stood motionless as they watched the screen, arms tight behind their backs.

The second, Professor An, the chief xenobiologist of the Terran Federation. Of Asian descent, he sat in a simple office on his university's campus, surrounded by precarious stacks of paper. Boer had a mixed impression of An. He had had a long career, the texture of his skin and thinness of his hair testament to the many expeditions and reports behind him. Boer could see an array of artifacts from different cultures and species displayed carefully behind him as he sat there, nervously fidgeting with the sleeve of his sweater. It was currently winter in Hong Kong, and he was dressed to fit. Slowly, a single strand became unraveled on the end, which he rolled between two fingers. Competency was assured with An. There was no better human when it came to speaking on other species, but something about An, about his mannerisms, had always struck her as ... vulnerable... during his classes. She wondered if he remembered her at all. She had always sat near the middle of the classroom and rarely spoke. She hadn't felt the need to.

The third, which Boer knew was joining them from the furthest away, was Representative Auckland. He was in about the same stage of his life as Fletcher, but was vastly different in temperament and appearance. Of Maori descent, Auckland had a relaxed nature to him as he rocked back and forth in the chair in his diplomatic office. Even so, he exuded from him a power and clarity, giving the impression that at a moment's notice he could turn to action. He was dressed as though he had just left some critical meeting. Of course, the current meeting had its own degree of importance. He sat slightly askew to the desk, looking off screen as one hand played idly in a bowl of soft green hard candies at the edge of his desk. Occasionally, he lifted one up and flicked it into his mouth, where it began its slow demise like its brethren prior. He was of a stocky build, a giant rectangle set to motion. A splash of the sharp white from the planet's star cut in from the side of the view, slicing its way through his office, far brighter than the light generated by Sol. Auckland, the chief representative of humanity on the Galactic Council, couldn't be pried from his duties. At any point, the Galactic Council could call a meeting, and he needed to remain on planet so that he could attend.

The five of them, Auckland, Coeur, An, Fletcher, and Boer, silently waited. The rest took Boer in, studying her youth, her inexperience, and weighed her. She could see their eyes sweeping over her through the camera. She wondered what thoughts passed through their minds. Here they were, the core members of humanity. The ones that shaped the path that humanity charted through the stars. How did this sudden intrusion of youth into their venerated halls make them feel? Would they resent her? Dismiss her? Boer didn't know.

No one spoke. They didn't need to. The meeting had not started yet. Once their final member joined, only then would they begin. They were all here, having been given their positions at her pleasure, the Terrarch.

When the sixth joined, they were first confronted by her seal, a black and white depiction of Earth, stark in its design. Divided down the middle, the colorations flipped from black for terrain and white for oceans to the opposite, showing the earth split in two by the sharp transition. A moment later, her ancient form flicked onto the screen. She was joining from a hospital bed, currently undergoing another treatment as the doctors continued to scrape yet more time with their beloved Terrarch. Occasionally, the edge of one of their forms would flit into view at the sides of the broadcast. Boer took in her form, the effects that the centuries had carved into her body, the valleys across her skin, the splotches of black and blue that highlighted her injections. Finally, Boer raised her gaze up to her eyes.

They were deep things, all pale and gray. When you gazed into them, they would latch onto you, drag you body and soul into their monumental depths. Boer could fold her short twenty four years into them, again and again, ten-fold, and still not fill their deep reservoir. Even through the screen, the Terrarch's eyes threatened to pull her into them, to envelop her and surround her with their power. That was her way.

"Fletcher," the Terrarch said tersely.

He stepped forward towards the conference table that he was standing at. "I have Gliese 667 C Beta's final report, transmitted via laser array shortly prior to the Xen'wa fleet's arrival, as well as the final report from the defensive AI in the

7

system. The Xen'wa fleet entered the system at approximately 1843 local time on SD 118323. One of their cruisers was set on a collision course with the station. They maintained silence as it approached. Before collision, they set a task for the DAI in the system. It proceeded to engage the Xen'wa fleet. It analyzed that it did not have the capabilities for complete repulsion of the force so it undertook an attritional stance, as planned. Over the following ten star dates, the DAI successfully led a number of feigning attacks and probes, exposing the various capabilities of Xen'wa design. It was successfully able to destroy or critically disable 138 of their vessels, totaling 12 cruisers, 28 destroyers, and four support ships. The remaining amount being composed of fighters. Coupled with the fourteen ships that suffered failures during their trip through deep space, that brings their total combat numbers to 482, though more ships are rip jumping in, including their flagship. The exact capabilities of their individual ships have been forwarded to your private terminal for further review. As of now, the remaining unmanned observation satellites in the system have yet to be located by the Xen'wa." With his task done, Fletcher stepped back, resuming his posture.

"Auckland?" came the Terrarch's sharp voice.

In his chair, he turned to face the terminal, looming over the edge of the desk. "The Xen'wa are already reporting to the council that this is a 'misunderstanding,' as they have coined it. The message that they are putting forth into the wider community is that their fleet was simply patrolling their borders when several of their ships suffered mechanical failures, namely the fourteen ships that they lost during transit through deep space. They state that when they arrived in the system, our defense forces immediately began assaulting them, despite mayday transmissions for aid."

The Terrarch looked at Fletcher. He quietly shook his head.

"They were unfortunately forced to return fire in defense of their vessels. All said and done, a large number of their ships were damaged by the aggressive and hostile actions of the

Terran forces. After combat ended, they immediately rendered aid to their own ships, but as the Terran ships offered no distress signals, they assumed all souls on board lost and left them adrift. Further, they are demanding compensation for this hostile act by the Terran Federation, namely these two systems."

He flicked his hand and two star charts appeared in the conference call. Boer looked them over. She recognized one was Gliese. The other's name she didn't recognize and didn't know much about it, just a string of letters and numbers.

"The Xen'wa state that upon receipt of these systems, they will retract all of their forces and cease hostilities. For the meantime, they will take up positions around the Gliese system until further notice. All of this is to be expected of course, but there was an interesting development."

The Terrarch raised an eyebrow.

"The Thlassians have offered to negotiate a settlement, as this is all occurring in their backyard." The Terrarch furrowed her brow. "Not their precise words, of course," Auckland added.

The gears immediately started turning in Boer's mind. The Thlassians were a small species. They had only joined the Galactic community some 25 years ago, shortly before Boer was born. If memory served, they had offered the translation devices that were now standard across the galaxy as their payment for membership of the council, though it took the council a further 22 years to accept them into their halls. She quickly keyed her terminal for more information. Their system only had three planets in orbit, one of which was habitable by them, their homeworld, Thlassia. The other two had been given a designation as near-habitable and potentially terraformable. As of yet, they had made no motions to do so. Their presence in space was minimal, as space travel was not something conducive to their aquatic biology.

As a result, in the twenty five years since they had joined, they had kept largely to themselves. Gliese itself directly bordered both Xen'wa space and the Thlassian home systems, both being a short hop via rip drive away. Perhaps this was their first attempt to secure a larger presence? No, that didn't feel right to Boer. She thought longer on them, the gears grinding and twisting in her mind. Slowly, an idea began to form. It was an audacious thing. Its arrogance ripped through her. She was unsure of it at first, but as more and more things started to slot in, a plan began to emerge from this bold idea. Despite its power, it was a desperate, fragile path. It could fail at any point. And the risk of it all… She realized she had been holding in her breath and let it shake its way out.

Once she had steadied herself, she looked back at the terminal. She wasn't sure when, but the conference had gone to silence. The rest of them sat there quietly, staring out of her screen with deep accusations.

"I'm sorry, I missed that last bit," she said, her cheeks burning in shame.

"Ambassador Boer, you missed nothing. Speak," the Terrarch said.

Boer felt as though the Terrarch's gaze was honed specifically on her as she took a deep breath and began. She laid it all out, every step, every twist, every turn. She explained just how far down they would dive. What pieces were needed. How they would contort the board. Just what she hoped they could achieve with the Xen'wa. When she reached the end, she fell silent, looking down in her lap, unable to bear the shame that filtered through her at the audacity of it. It was too foolish, too naive, too bold, risked too much. She had known this before she even spoke. She had disappointed the Terrarch. There was no way that she would assent to it. Boer was not ready. It had been foolish to hope that she was.

Boer glanced back up at the monitor. In Fletcher's form, she could see a grim determination. He understood the potential costs of it all, felt the weight of it. Boer knew that he would feel the need to act, to stop her from causing such turmoil. Professor An's eyes had gone wide in terror, a cold fear slicing its way through his body. He appeared as though some animal of prey, frozen in fear as death descended upon him. Her shame was confirmed when she looked at Auckland. He had his eyes closed, head down and was chuckling at just how young and inexperienced she was. She couldn't bear to look at the Terrarch, to see the disappointment in her eyes. It was her that would cut the deepest. Boer spiraled into the darkness for a moment before the light came once more.

"I will send the Xen'wa and Thlassians my message," came the Terrarch's voice, wrenching its way through Boer's mind. "An, send her your full report on the Thlassians. The original version. It's the better of the two. The rest of you, fully read her in. She needs the entire picture before we finalize the plan. I want her to have everything, even my private files. I want a full report on the details as soon as possible."

The Terrarch cut her transmission.

Later that day, Boer finished drafting her plan. The information that Auckland and Fletcher had given her on the Thlassians was... deeply unsettling. She was hopeful, mind you, but it was troubling regardless. In a way, it validated her initial observations on the Xen'wa. As she typed up the final words, she braced herself before she sent it out into the world. It quickly made its way to the main parties involved. They spent their time with it, measured it. Throughout the day, they would make their notes. Write their suggestions.

Then they were supposed to send the plan back with their revisions. The first she expected entirely. Boer had gotten his measure. An had no revisions for the plan. He couldn't formulate them. Instead, he had sent her a desperate thing. An appeal to her humanity. Don't do this thing. The risk was far too great. It would be the end of everything. We simply couldn't. On and on the arguments went. He must have spent the entirety of the night writing them until he had nothing left to plead. The final line of the document was but a single word.

Please.

Boer ignored him. She had to.

She understood him, though. As horrible as the original idea had been, when she had been read into the Terrarch's secrets, it had only grown worse. It was a dangerous gamble. It may have a wondrous reward. Besides, she had only suggested it. It hadn't been her decision. It wasn't hers to bear. The Terrarch is the one who made the decision, the one who *actually* set things into motion. If anyone was to bear the burden, it was her.

She tried to convince herself of that. Tried to persuade herself that it was the Terrarch who would bear the responsibility for all the risk and the danger.

Somehow she couldn't. Deep down inside, she knew the truth. The violence of the plan was her responsibility. She was the one that had birthed it into being. It would be her burden to bear. That thought alone was what caused her to temper it as she began the second draft.

She recalled the file that Fletcher had brought, personally. He wasn't allowed to leave it. She had to turn off all electronics, including her eye, while she read it. It came in a simple folder. Fletcher explained that it was one of three copies, all of which were closely monitored. When Boer read it, she had trembled. For a moment, she had actually considered using it, but then she realized that it would be too great a betrayal to what they were trying to be. She opted to not include it in her plans. Fletcher had taken it away shortly thereafter. Even so, the memory of it echoed in her mind. Even now, it tempted her with its seductive evil. It would have simplified everything instantly, but would have cost all that they were trying to achieve. It did however allow her perspective, the chance to back away from the edge that the initial plan had rested on.

She took in the observations of those that had offered them, then finalized the plan and sent it out.

Afterwards, the only other person to send modifications to the plan sent her message. It was mostly minor tweaks, a small change here and there, soft delicate touches driven by her vast experience.

She did, however, have a whole section in regards to names.

The plan was complete.

The following day, Boer woke up from her slumber with a startle. She stayed like that for a moment, body supported by her arms as she hovered over her pillow and recalled the extent to which she had gone. Just how far down the well she had suggested they go. A bead of sweat dropped off her brow, wetting the pillow beneath her.

Her dreams hadn't been simple things. She dreamed of lost loves and lives, entire societies torn asunder. Planets shattering. Limbless torsos with electronic eyes, blood pouring from where their jaw should be. Throughout all of it, Professor An leveled his accusation, a single finger outstretched towards her.

"Monster!"

She flopped back down on her pillow, letting out a small protestation into its comforting embrace. A large part of her wanted to stay there, wrapped in the nurturing warmth of her covers, but she knew that would be an avoidance, cowering in her bed to shirk her duties. When she finally turned her head in the morning light, hair splaying out in every direction as it rubbed against the pillow, Boer saw that her terminal was beeping with a message. She thought about just laying there one more time, in the safe and warm embrace of her bed. Eventually, she submitted to the day and rose.

It wasn't often one had a private meeting with the Terrarch. Most people went their entire lives without ever laying eyes on their leader in person. She was far too busy for any scheduled thing, yet people worked out ways to find her. For most of those who did get the pleasure of laying eyes on her, it was only in passing, having waited out for the opportunity to glimpse her as she walked by. Most commonly, as she was either going to or returning from treatment. Some cheered. Some cried. Some stood in silence as they took in the form of the one who had brought humanity so very far forward and the burden that her mantle had ravaged across her form. These moments were things that people carried with them, cherished.

It was rarer still for people to be able to honestly say they had spoken to her, held an actual conversation. Most people only knew her through her broadcasts, messages out to humanity as she shaped the zeitgeist. Boer thought of the first time that she had spoken with her. It had happened a long time ago, when Boer was just a child.

It was not a happy time.

She had been surrounded by tubes and monitors, doctors in their scrubs, scalpels as they dove down towards her. Pain had wracked her body and half of her world had gone dark, even still, the doctors had come to her and said they needed to take more. And they did.

No, she thought. *It was not a happy time.*

It had been a time of great despair and pain for Boer. The type of pain that would lay a small child out on an operating table, drill down and twist and pull and wrench everything out from them, until they were nothing but a great empty cavity where once had been joy and happiness. The type of pain that would plunge half of the world in darkness, just to make the other blind to the joys of the light.

It was then that the Terrarch had come to her, donned in the same loose fitting soft blue gowns wrapped around her form that she herself had been dressed in. The Terrarch had come to her and embraced her, and now it was her turn to do the same.

Boer steeled herself, and stepped out of the car that had brought her here from her apartment.

14

The Terrarch sat alone, over at the edge of the park. It wasn't a popular destination. It carried too much emotion to it now. Most sought to avoid it, to try and forget. Some succeeded. A few, though, a few remembered and learned from the lesson.

When it had been first constructed, it was a place of great joy and happiness, a place where families gathered and celebrated, where love was professed and shared. There was a time when you would have had to arrive early, lest all the best spots be filled. Those joys didn't last.

As the centuries had passed, it had become a memorial, a mausoleum. A reminder of what mankind had done, of their foolish blindness. A place of mourning.

Boer slowly walked across the park, her footsteps echoing in the silence and approached the water's edge. Without saying a word, she sat on the bench beside the Terrarch, joining her as she gazed out across the oceans that humanity had killed. They sat like that for a while, each diving down into their own thoughts.

Boer recalled something that the Terrarch had shared with her. A memory of a beautiful world beneath a floating child, full of life, color, and cheer. It had been given to Boer as a single drop of joy that fell into her great well of darkness, before exploding into a great calamitous wave that flowed its way back up, carrying the small child with it. She wondered what it must have been like, to have so much life around you, gazing up at the strange creature that floated above them while it gazed down and thought the same. A great gift from a great and kind person.

"You should send someone else," Boer said quietly. "Someone more experienced. I cannot do this for you."

Boer dropped her eyes. Silently, the Terrarch took in Boer's shame and doubts into herself, and acted. Boer saw the Terrarch extend one arm. It hung in the air alone towards her. She watched as it trembled slightly in the air with the effort. Boer exhaled her emotions out and took it, their two hands twined together, resting on the bench.

"I trust you to deliver our message."

CHAPTER TWO

"You ask what it means to recognize another? First, look deep into the mirror. Take in your form, your eyes, your face, your body. Now look past it, see your flesh laid bare and vulnerable. Take in the scars and marks that time has driven into you. Look past it. See the hopes, the dreams, the fears, the turmoil and ecstasy that made you. Only once you truly see it, truly understand it, can you ever hope to recognize it."

-- Wisdoms of the Terrarch

The deck beneath Boer's feet shuddered and rumbled as the last of the waves of gravity that had flung her so deeply into space petered out, the shuttle's rip drive finally spooling down. She watched as the screens in the shuttle flickered green in confirmation. Shortly later, the whole deck lurched as the sublight engines engaged and pushed them on their journey.

Boer's shuttle made its way down from space towards the blue jewel that was Thlassia. Despite how far away it was from the Sol system, it was remarkably Earth-like. From the small display monitors that rested in front of her pilot, Boer could see large swatches of fluffy white cloud stretched across the horizons, great mountains of moisture that were suspended high in the atmosphere of the planet betraying the massive storms that could ravage their way across the planet.

It rested perfectly in the Goldilocks zone of its star, a G-type yellow dwarf star, just like our own Sol. Its atmosphere was also so incredibly similar to ours. There were a few differences of course: the lowered portion of nitrogen resting at just above 48%, the presence of neon, and the fact that the level of oxygen was barely higher than on earth. All of this was of little concern.

The air was breathable, both for her and the Xen'wa Ambassador, though her counterpart would have to return to his orbital shuttle so his body could offgas the neon daily. Even now, her sensors picked up Ambassador Stresi's shuttle making its descent alongside hers. Its design was vastly different from her own. The Terran shuttles were utilitarian constructs, meant to get from one place to the other as quickly as possible, little more than boxes that made their way through the stars. The Xen'wa shuttle much resembled their own form, that of a swooping bird poised to strike. It was a thing of sharp, yet elegant lines.

When both of the ambassadors had landed on opposite ends of the massive pad, purpose built by the Thlassians to facilitate the talks, they began their journey down and into the diplomatic offices. Boer was immediately struck by the dense humidity of the planet. It was a water world, afterall.

Reaching the end of their respective ramps, shoes and talons on the tarmac, the two turned and looked across the distance that separated them, a massive stretch that could have easily fit fifty of their shuttles. They stood like that a while, each taking in the other's form over that great distance. Boer couldn't make out much of his features. She had been briefed that Xen'wa sight was substantially better than her own, evolved to see the great distances involved when soaring above your prey.

To Boer, Ambassador Stresi's form was too small to make out in fine detail, however, she could see the overall avian trend to his features, the puffed chest that he held before him, the wings folded neatly behind his back. As he had walked down the ramp, she had taken in the bobbing motion in which he moved, how he splayed out the talons on his feet to anchor his position. They continued to stare at each other for a good while. Eventually, when both were satisfied, they stepped forward to their respective elevators and began their descents.

When the elevator finally opened, Boer hurried through the halls, briefly stopping at the small chambers the Thlassian's had built for her. She didn't take any time to examine them, simply opening the door and setting the satchels that she had brought with her into the suite before turning to leave. She had to get to the orientation with the Thlassian ambassador.

Prior to any negotiations, both parties were to spend scheduled time with the Thlassian ambassador to learn how to use and interact with their new translator system. The Thlassians had indicated that they would like to have the orientation with both of the species, but the Terrarch had declined.

Instead, the Terrarch had insisted that they do them separately, one after the other. Immediately, the question was asked which would go first. Another battle was beginning to brew over this simple question before the Thlassians had shifted the negotiation by simply stating they would do it in order of distance. Whoever's homeworld was closest would go first, the other would wait until they were done. Thus, it was Boer who found herself standing outside the simple door that led to the diplomatic chamber first.

Despite its plain details, no engravings or decorations of any kind, a simple gray with a slight amount of green in the metal, the door carried a substantial weight to it. The only direct contact that she would have with her counterpart from the Xen'wa was going to be in the room that lay beyond. She was allowed messages of text, but nothing more. Boer knew that once she stepped inside, everything would start, the plan would be in motion. She breathed in a deep breath, held it a moment, before raising her hand and activating the door. It hissed loudly as it rose to the ceiling.

When Boer entered the diplomatic chamber, a tremor tore its way through her body from the sight of the Thlassian

Ambassador's form.

He resided in a great tank that Boer could see had a small circular door at its back. The entire thing was set diagonally in the corner of the room, great metal bracings attaching it to the sides of the chamber. Ambassador Gwooon's main body, a large ovoid pod, was easily three meters in length. He had two eyes, the pupils a dark, ominous black that spoke of untold depths as they twisted and waved. They were mounted in an opposable socket, allowing him to turn and focus them separately. Along the length of his main body ran a simple frill, small flecks of brilliant green occasionally breaking the otherwise uniform gray, tinted with the slightest blue. Beneath him, a bundle of arms and tentacles almost the same size as him twisted and writhed. Most of them were thin, nimble things, however the tentacles, one on each side of his body, were far larger, and Boer could see that these alone had a ridge of suction cups running down their length to where they ended in a large flat portion. Two small jets twisted and turned, letting out the occasional bubble as they pulsed in and out.

All said, he looked remarkably like a cuttlefish, a tiny creature that had once lived in Earth's oceans in the distant past, back when they could still support life. His size though, his size made it as though he were pulled directly out of one of the old horror films, with just a flick of his tentacles, smashing the glass and dragging her into the tank then further out into the water where her body would twist and writhe as it struggled vainly on.

And she would struggle.

She would first try to evade and dodge, but when that failed, she would reach out and grab a shard of glass from the shattered tank, cutting and slashing her way through that massive form, desperate to get as far from it as she could, but it would be no use against something such as that.

Boer pushed the errant thoughts from her mind, dismissing the senseless fear as it worked its way down her spine. She saw a small yellow light begin at the tip of Ambassador Gwooon's arms, then slowly flicker its way up and over his main body. A deep noise came from him, another haunting echo of something that once occurred on Earth.

Based on An's reports of their anatomy, their primary mode of speech consisted of two large air bladders that were connected by their vocal cords. They made their speech by running the air from one bladder to the other, vibrating their vocal cords along the way. The translator box that was mounted to the front of the tank came to life.

"Greetings, Ambassador Boer," it said simply.

The voice it used was highly robotic, zero inflection to the interpretation. The entire translation process was rather quick, though it didn't outstrip any of the Terran translators that had been developed. In fact, it was noticeably slower. The Thlassians had said that they were working on a new translator that would be developed in tandem with the negotiations. Boer wasn't sure that this was a particularly good idea. She found such an auspicious moment as helping to negotiate a peace between two factions a non-ideal time to debut an unproven bit of tech, but here they were. The Thlassians had indicated that they wanted to try this new version, one that could potentially "lead to greater understanding," as they had phrased it. Neither side particularly wanted to scuttle the talks, so both had assented.

Boer finally pulled her gaze off of Gwooon and took in the rest of the room. She knew what she would find. It was a simple room, a large cube in which there were only three things. Bare and clinical. Towards the door from which Stresi would enter, a simple metal bar upon which he could roost. Its height had been of great debate while they negotiated conditions for the talks. Stresi had wanted it higher, so that it would be a more natural roost for him. The Terrarch had firmly denied that. If the talks were to happen, they needed to be done in a way that did not put Stresi in the position of power at all times, looming over Boer like some great hawk about to swoop down upon its prey and tear her to pieces. As it was, when he was resting upon it, his eyes would be level with Boer's only if she stood. She still had some misgivings towards that, but she hadn't felt scuttling the talks worth the fight.

Towards her side, a simple metal table, completely spartan in its design paired with a singular chair of equal nature. It had no decorations or inlays of any kind. Boer didn't want it to be a distraction, but she had insisted that it be provided. It was a vital component to Terran negotiations, she had said.

"Greetings to you, Ambassador Gwooon. On behalf o..." She could get no further before the device cut her off with a loud BOO-BOOP. She fell to silence. Her brow furrowed as she wondered why the translator had cut her off so early. She barely had spoken any words when it had loudly beeped, shutting her down. Surely the translators could handle larger swatches of words than that spare amount.

Once more the haunting echoes came from Gwooon's form. The translator absorbed the sounds, then repeated it for Boer so that she could understand. "If you would, define the last word you used. State 'Translator - Add' before doing so."

Boer turned and looked at him. Taking in his form, she was unable to assign any emotion, he was far too alien for that. However, she did get the sense that as much as she was taking him in, he was equally watching and analyzing her. She paused, trying to think back to the word she used. She then thought her way through to the simplest, straightest definition she could.

"Uhh... Translator - Add: Behalf - for someone else." She fell once more to silence, thoughts running through her mind.

Another loud echo reverberated from the tank.

"Continue," he intoned, flicking one of his arms slightly towards her.

She started up again. "On behalf of the Terrarch, we thank you..." BOO-BOOP. This time, Boer knew why. She thought about what she said and only a small part of her was surprised. Boer thought to herself a moment, trying to distill all that was that word down as far as she could. Realizing that it would depend on too many other topics, she was unsure if she should go with something literal. Hesitantly, she spoke.

"Ambassador Gwooon, what if the word used is not easily

defined?"

"Ambassador Boer, do what you can. You may add context or a situation in which it may be used."

She gave him a quick nod, before realizing that he might not understand the gesture. "Translator - Add: Thank - to express appreciation?" she said, her voice trending upwards as she was unsure if the translator would accept it. When it didn't beep at her, she pressed onwards. "Said when one person has received something from the other." A thought crossed her mind. She wondered if the translator could handle it. It would certainly be more useful if it could. "Part of a larger concept called gratitude, the process of going out of your way to show appreciation for what people have done." The translator didn't beep at her. It accepted it. Boer waited a moment, then Gwooon spoke.

"Thank you," he said simply. Boer stared at him for a moment, eyes wide and blinking. Sensing something important about the moment, Gwooon continued. "We have a word for it. We didn't know you had a parallel."

Ah, so that was it, Boer thought to herself, before pressing onwards. "On behalf of the Terrarch, I would like to thank you for hosting these neutral grounds at w..." BOO-BOOP.

What? Surely they have a word for ground! All species had one. Then Boer thought to herself a moment, and she saw the problem. The word had multiple meanings in her own language. Here, she was using it adjacently to its definition, but not literally. It expressed the slightest expansion of thought that the translator did not have the context for.

"Translator - Add... Alternate Definition: Grounds - Area." Her voice had raised, questioning the addition to the command, but it hadn't caused an issue. The translator accepted it. Very well then. She was getting the hang of this. The translator could not only have words added to it, but it could also have alternate meanings and contexts and it would sort them out.

"The Terrarch would like to express thanks ..." She paused a moment, testing out the usage switch. It didn't beep. "...

for hosting these neutral grounds so that we all might move forward."

Gwooon floated there, staring at her. There was almost something expectant about that stare. It was so foreign to her, yet she recognized something profound about it. Gwooon seemed as though he were waiting for something from her. She had delivered the greeting that they had crafted, and yet Gwooon felt as though he wanted something more.

A realization swept through her, sparked by something that she had, in a flash, recognized. It shook her to her very core, causing her perspective to shift. A new possibility had opened, Boer could feel it. She must inform the Terrarch immediately. They would have to update the plan.

"Translator - Add: You're Welcome - A traditional reply given when someone expresses thanks. It is used to convey that said thanks were well-received and appreciated," she softly added.

"You're welcome."

She walked through the small hallway quickly, headed towards the personal chambers that the Thlassians had constructed for her. They had talked for a few minutes longer, exchanging the formalities and reaffirming the terms at which these talks would be hosted. But none of that mattered in the moment. She hurriedly pressed the soft buttons that controlled the door to her suite. In her haste, her mind was aswim with the echoes of An's report, the phrase "a depth of emotion and understanding that haunted," reverberated again and again.

Prior to her meeting with Gwooon, she had only had time to drop her belongings off into the entrance before needing to go meet him. She marched deeper into the suite than before, only grabbing her briefcase as she entered. She didn't even have time to thoroughly examine her surroundings before she quickly pulled out her terminal, placing it on the small counter that separated the living quarters from the cooking area. Her fingers flew across the keyboard. She had to enter her credentials three times, hands trembling with each keystroke. The final attempt she was under warning of a lockout, but she managed to enter her login and password successfully. Quickly, she opened up a communication stream.

As far away from Earth she was, it was text only for most communications. The conference that had started this whole endeavor had been exorbitantly expensive to send down the quantum relays. It had been needed at the time, and Auckland had a dedicated video bandwidth allotment that they had used. Any video conferences had to be precleared to ensure that the network wasn't already being tasked with some other critical transmission.

Terrarch?

In front of the mirror. Now.

Boer quickly stood up, not even bothering to log herself off, a massive breach of data security, but she hadn't the time. She needed to show the Terrarch. The Terrarch needed to understand.

She quickly walked over to the connected bathroom and stood in front of the full body mirror that the Terrarch had insisted upon. The Xen'wa had assumed her species was vain for doing so, but Boer understood why now. She stood there, in front of the mirror, her body still enflamed by her realization. She felt her implanted eye begin to emit a very slight hum in its berth, something the scientist had briefed her was someone dialing into it. She stood there, motionless other than the heavy breaths that were shuddering through her body as she stared at her reflection.

A moment later, her ear buzzed and the Terrarch sent a message, distorted, much as the difference between how one thought they sounded versus a recording.

"I had hoped."

CHAPTER THREE

"Do not hide behind a shield. You should always lay yourself bare for the world to see. Allow yourself to shine so that others may see your splendor. Do not cover it in a desperate attempt to save yourself. That shield has a far better use. Protecting the one beside you so that they too may shine."

-- Wisdoms of the Terrarch

———————————————————————————————

Back on Earth, Professor An sat alone in his office. He had his head down on his desk, arms crossed before him to provide cushion against the hardwood. He was deep in thought, a thousand possibilities and threats tearing their way through his mind.

An had tried. He honestly did. But he couldn't just stand idly by. Too much was at risk. It wasn't just his own species that was caught up in the massive web they wanted to spin. If it was that alone, it would have crushed him but he would have accepted it. He spun in his chair, looking at the artifacts he had gathered over a lifetime of study.

In his collection, he had collected sixteen of the seventeen recognized species of high intelligence and capability, members of the Galactic Council. He had artifacts from some of the earliest religions of the Xen'wa, back when they still referred to themself as 'The ones who rode the storm,' in their language. He had artifacts of the Scretta, spears and swords from their first star hunt when they were still the ravagers of the universe, desperate to find another world to pillage. He had bits and ends from all of the species, reminders of the humble and often wretched origins from which all of the species had started in their infancies.

But the community had grown.

Yes, the Council wasn't perfect. Not by any stretch of the imagination. What Boer intended to do, however... That wasn't growth. It was destruction, pure and simple. It would be the end of all that he had loved, all that he had cherished and learned over the course of his life. It was horrendous, monstrous even.

When he thought of all the time he had spent learning from the other cultures of the Council, he despaired. He knew he needed to stop it, but An had no immediate way of seeing that borne into truth.

How could he?

The Terrarch was the most powerful, influential human alive. No, that had ever existed. And Boer... Boer was a psychopath. Only someone with such a condition could possibly have come up with something so very violent, so cruel and evil. He reflected on the short time that she had spent in her classroom, nearly six years ago now. Had she shown signs of her psychopathy even then?

An sat like that, drowning in his despair, thinking about the horrendous savagery that the humans would be sending out as a message out into the galaxy. They might as well send a message to all with a giant flashing sign that said "Hey, look here! We're the biggest monsters existence has ever given birth to!"

He thought about sending a warning, blowing the whole thing up. He knew it wouldn't help though. Not enough of the galaxy would hear the message. Most would discard it. An wasn't well known across the systems. Why would he be? He was just a researcher of species. Only a few would actually listen to him. Besides, it would take far too long to spread. That was the ultimate cruelty of it all. The whole plan was so bloody violent that it would be completely resolved within thirty star dates once it started. An unfathomable number.

In thirty star dates, humanity would either be dead, or would have repeated the past and tried to impose their culture onto everyone else, violently and without consideration.

An understood what would happen after. History showed it. One only had to open a book of the past to know the course that humanity was now charting in the stars, a repeat of what had once happened on Earth. They would supplant themselves as the foremost force in the galaxy. There would be an entirely new structure of power, and humanity would step in and take the reins. Boer might not even intend for it to happen, but it would. It wouldn't be something done out of malice, but out of shortage and necessity. There would be something that was required, and it would at first come as a request. Faced with the implicit barbarity of the Terrans, they would acquiesce. The requests would be simple at first, but eventually, *eventually*, they would cement the master-servant relationship more formally. It might not be this generation, it might not be for a hundred, or even two hundred years, but it *would* happen. Boer would be responsible for the great wave of colonialism in space. It may not be a military domination, perhaps an economic or technological one, but it *would* happen.

He *must* stop Boer. It was the only way to save the rest. He had pleaded with her, begged, debased himself in front of her will, and she had ignored him. Had ignored HIM, the personal xenologist of the Terrarch, the foremost scholar of all of the cultures of the galaxy, the foremost expert on all of the value of the other species.

An dwelled on it throughout the next day.

Boer had already departed for the Thlassian world, so a direct attack was out. So the question had become how could he possibly attack a plan as mental as what she had proposed? He ran several scenarios through his head. On his terminal, the unopened file of Boer's second draft rested menacingly on the screen. He hadn't the strength to look at it and see what additional evils she had wormed into it.

He continued to weigh possibilities in his mind. He had a few connections with some of the species. If he gathered enough of them, maybe that could sway the situation. Maybe they could get word to the council and then the council could act, do something that would be enough to convince them that this wasn't actually a valid option. He could take away the choice all together. *Yes,* he thought to himself, *That is the way this must go.*

He had begun typing in his first message when it happened.

The terminal beeped.

Immediately, the screen changed to the Terrarch's seal, the black and white of the sigil stark on the screen. It wouldn't respond to any of his keystrokes or commands. It was simply a lump of plastics and metals before him now. An's eyes went wide in terror.

A single message suddenly replaced it on his screen, opening itself to display its death sentence prominently for him. An looked over it and felt a different kind of despair take over his being.

It was all gone. All of it. With a few clicks of the keys, the Terrarch had taken everything away from him. He looked up. Campus security had already arrived to help carry out the Terrarch's will. An despaired, not knowing where he would end up.

They were not gentle with him.

First thing they did upon entering the room was to slam him to his desk, face flat against the papers that were on top. Immediately, they began working their way around the room, gathering all the objects around. Carefully, they started putting them into boxes and more and more of the security started to pour into the room, far more than was needed for someone like An. They went through everything. He tried to struggle, tried to resist, but they just held him there, moving about his office with ruthless efficiency. They scoured everything. Every artifact, every scrap of paper, anything that was larger than a paperclip.

Every piece that he had gathered over his venerable career now fit neatly into boxes.

They took it all and hauled them away. It was all gone. Everything that he remembered his achievements by, everything that spoke to his journey through the stars, was boxed up and gone. He tried to resist it. Of course, he had. However, when they clicked the handcuffs around his wrists, he knew there was no point.

It was already all gone.

His head hung in defeat, he was led quietly out of the room.

On the observation deck of the *TSS Destiny's Spear*, the flagship of the Terran Defense Fleet, Admiral Fletcher watched the commotion that was all around his charge. The Terrarch had seen fit to see to a few modifications to the vessel. The first was a change to one of the interdiction craft it carried. Mounted on the exterior of the behemoth, the interdiction crafts were AI controlled. All the crew had to do was launch them and set them to a task and they performed their role admirably. They had been instructed to add crew quarters and life support systems enough to sustain ten souls for a few days. It had also been redubbed the *TSS Stiletto.* Its pair on the other side had also been redubbed the *TSS Misericorde,* though it had received no additions. They normally were unnamed ships, only designated by their identification number.

Apt names, given their purpose, Fletcher thought to himself as he watched one of the other additions, a large detachable extension that would adhere to the bow of his ship for the time being, slowly drift into position before its great arms stretched out to cradle the *Destiny*. It was a ship in its own right, capable of a rip jump. The rip generator on it had been tuned to be extra violent. For the time being, it would sit placidly on the front of the *Destiny*, along for the ride through the stars. It had three long extensions that anchored to the *Destiny,* carefully so they would not damage the hull. They swept down towards a central hub that housed most of the important bits, including the rip generator.

He accepted it. It was ballsy. A part of him kinda respected it.

The other five ships, however, Fletcher had drawn a line. He had been worried that he would be overruled, maybe even replaced. However, when he notified the Terrarch that he would not allow those ships a direct connection to the *Destiny*, the Terrarch had acquiesced without comment. He had thought that she might put up more resistance, but they had settled with the other five syncing up and joining the *Destiny* for rip jumps. They would not connect and interface directly. The defense AI on board the *Destiny* would maintain their positioning around the ship, remotely.

Now, all around the *Destiny*, the five smaller ships floated menacingly. Their forms could only be called barebones, the rapid result of Terran design and construction. The engineers, after getting over their initial shock at the request, had only taken a few hours to come up with the design. Despite the abhorrent nature of their purpose, they didn't need too much complexity. It had taken a fair bit longer to build, but still well within the timeframe so that they would be ready before they were needed. Still, Fletcher despised them. Everything that they lacked was a testament to their vile purpose.

They had nothing in the way of protection.

They didn't need it.

There were no quarters on them for crew of any kind.

Their purpose didn't necessitate it.

They were things of violence incarnate. Their purpose was so very simple and straightforward. They consisted of a singular shaft, down which Fletcher could see dozens of rip drives, each far larger than would be needed to accomplish a rip for a ship of that size. Each was tuned to cause maximum gravitational distortion. Maximum.

The 'head' of these barbaric monstrosities was a massive pyramid, the base of which stretched well past the rest of the ship out into space. The rear was a massive block of engines, enough thrust to get them well into relativistic flight, close to the speed of light. The entirety of the ships, wherever possible, was constructed out of an alloy called CrCoNi, a super dense and durable material.

Fletcher heard the sharp steps of his second in command coming towards him. He didn't turn to her, his eyes transfixed to the aberrations that were approaching his ship. Decades of serving alongside one another had made it so that the man could recognize his second's approach by the sound of her gait alone.

"Sir," she said. He turned to Vice-Admiral Coeur, and returned the salute that he had known was there before he looked. "Synchronization of the Crocketts is on schedule to complete at 0833. All other assets are already secured and ready for rip." Since the crew had been briefed on them, they had started to refer to the five ships as "Crocketts," in reference to the materials from which they had been constructed as well as an old weapons system from the Earth's past, one that was borne into being by the same violence and desperation that humanity was now considering birthing once more.

Fletcher looked up into her eyes.

"Vice-Admiral Coeur." She saluted once more, and turned to return to Command. Before she left, Admiral Fletcher added one more thing.

"Coeur!"

She turned, looking back to where he was standing. She took in his grim expression, shared in his burden for but the briefest of moments, before she saw his expression harden into something more fervorous.

"Don't refer to them as assets again. Cargo will suffice." His voice was terse and strained. Coeur let out a deep breath of understanding. A tension that she had been carrying left her. Fletcher knew that she would have been harboring a similar thought. They had served alongside each other for far too long for him to have not understood that. Without waiting for her reply, he turned back up to where the Crocketts floated.

No, Fletcher would not allow them to connect directly to his ship.

To do so would sully it.

Humanity had stepped out into the stars with one goal. Peace. The *TSS Destiny's Spear*, while the epitome of all of the Terran Federation's military prowess, was not intended for the spreading of war and violence. Its primary role: interdiction. Its task was to respond to any threats and hostilities, defensively. Humanity had long since learned the lessons of its violent past. They understood where it would push them. And so, they had strived for something different. Yearned for it. They were desperate to achieve it.

Fletcher looked up at the five ships: *King, Queen, Bishop, Rook,* and *Knight.*

He honestly didn't know if they had.

Alone in her hospital bed, the Terrarch rubbed one hand across her brow and severed the visual connection with Fletcher.
She understood.

After Fletcher got the final confirmation that the 'cargo' was synced and ready to go, he made his way to the core of the ship, Command. Buried deep in the infrastructure of the vessel, it was the beating heart of the *Destiny*. In it, he could see that his crew was already focused to task. He didn't feel the need to say anything. Instead, he walked up to Vice-Admiral Coeur.

"Sir, the ship is ready to launch. All crew are aboard and the 'cargo' is in position and synced," she said, adhering to his earlier request. As always, Coeur was the epitome of professionalism and ability. Fletcher was fortunate to have had her as his second.

"Very well, Vice-Admiral Coeur, Command is yours, take us out."

CHAPTER FOUR

"Do not focus on beginnings and ends. It is human nature to do so, but it is an injustice. Life is not some sudden and sharp thing. It is a gradual continuum. More than just the beginning matters. More than just the end. Every step, every action, every choice, treat them all as they matter and are of importance. After all, if you take out a single piece of the puzzle, then it is no longer complete. A single link in the phalanx, and it falters."

-- Wisdoms of the Terrarch

L ightyears away, the Xen'wa Representative continued his rant for the council.

"... and so our fleet shall remain in the system until the Terrans provide just recompense!" the Xen'wa representative shouted, finally bringing it to an end.

Auckland let out a sigh, unhooking the Terran-built translator from his ear. It was not like the Thlassian design. It was only capable of picking up what few languages that it had been programmed for. In addition, it only translated into Terran. It didn't have the capabilities to facilitate transfer back and forth. Auckland still preferred using it, however, to listen. There was something familiar about it, comforting. He was a creature of habit, afterall. He enjoyed his small comforts. The Terran translators were something that he had been trained on over forty years ago when he had first assumed this position.

The Thlassian translators had only made their way to these chambers five years ago. The other species had adopted them quickly, discarding their own personalized devices in favor of the Thlassian's. Despite their adoption, Auckland still didn't rely on the Thlassian device fully. His reason for this was simple. It allowed him moments like this, where he could press the dialogue without having to wait for it to finish out its translations for all of the species. He enjoyed the violence of it.

Auckland stood up, a light coming on above him to signify that he was being recognized.

"And as we have said before, there will be no recompense! Your ships entered the system *illegally* with hostile intent!" He didn't know why he bothered with the inflections. The translators wouldn't relay it. Something in him made him do it, add those little flairs that his mind, no, *soul,* made him weave into his speech.

"Intent?" the Xen'wa representative retorted. Auckland now had to wait for the translator, but it didn't matter. The entire interruption had been a maneuver, a calculated thing to help control the narrative of the talks.

"There was no intent. It was simply a matter of expediency. Our ships had suffered catastrophic failures while in deep space. Your system was merely the closest. We have said it before and will say it again. This 'misunderstanding,'" Auckland tsked, "was not our desire."

"Do you truly expect us to believe that? Your closest system is fifty cycles by sublight. Even so, you could have rip jumped a ship out there to provide aid."

"The ships in question were on a long term patrolling mission. They encountered technical issues. They made the decision that your system was the best course of action to resolve an emergent issue and headed there."

"And not Thlassia? It was closer."

"Thlassia did not have what we required!"

Auckland was about to spring the trap. He had guided the Xen'wa representative directly to it and the avian had flown headfirst in.

"And there it is." He said, extending a finger to the Xen'wa. "What. Was. Required! That is what this is all about. You saw a greater prize and decided to send your ships there. Gliese is ours. It was part of our original concessions when we first joined the council. Admit it, this is all a desperate attempt to develop some form of legal claim for another system!" Of course it was. Auckland didn't need to hear his response to know. This wasn't the first time that something like this had happened.

"They are ours. We will do with them what we see fit." Auckland narrowed his eyes as his voice filled with vitriol. "And handing them over to the Xen'wa is not a part of that."

None of this was truly meant for the Xen'wa representative, of course. It was intended for others, which each listened to their own translation of what was being said. He looked across the room, his eyes passing over the fifteen other species present. Most of the members of the council were from smaller species, some physically, some not. Either way, the focus and discussions of the council tended to be dominated by the concerns of the three species that had the largest confirmed fleets. A species could be facing a world-wide famine, but it wouldn't matter if they ranked fifteenth in military size. Instead, the conversation would be dominated by trade agreements concerning the most mind-numbing of minutiae and tedium. The Galactic Council, for all its blusterings about, 'unity' and 'common good' was a callous and capricious thing. Each race had joined the council with a proffer, some form of technology that they gave to the council to secure their memberships. That wasn't the extent of the price they paid for being here.

As far as Auckland was concerned, the council had a fatal flaw. Things like what the Xen'wa were trying to do happened all too frequently. It was far too common of an occurrence for one of the larger species to use their fleet to bully one of the smaller. Often, there would be some trumped up reason as to why, the barest of excuses for the hostile actions taken. Sometimes though, if the species were just small enough, what was wanted would just be taken instead, all pretense completely abandoned.

What could they do? Lodge a protest? The council wouldn't recognize them. Refuse to yield? They would only lose more as the hostile fleets descended upon them. Auckland found the whole process abhorrent. He hated his work here, but he also understood its importance and that he was the best man for the job, despite his loathing of the entire system.

Auckland didn't like bullies. The Terrarch recognized this.

Of course, that is what the Xen'wa were trying to do. The Xen'wa were the third largest species on the council, in terms of confirmed Fleet size and territorial holdings. The Terrans were eighth. In addition, the Xen'wa were expansionist. If it came to it, they could just declare war and take the systems. There would be some hemming and hawwing about it on the council, but they would turn their blind eyes to it and refuse to intervene. The Xen'wa were bigger. They were worth more. Fortunately, the Terrans had bolstered a defense against this very thing from happening.

The only thing stopping this from escalating was the rip drives. The drives were the only way of avoiding relativistic flight to get between the stars, a prospect which could add decades or even centuries by Terran reckoning. As one approached the speed of light, time began to 'desync' with your surroundings. Sure, this benefited the lifespans of the crew of the ship, being able to cover vast distances over weeks or months, but it came at a heavy cost. From their perspective, the world around them sped up. On the ship, only a week could pass, but when they decelerated, they would find everyone that they had ever known or loved dead and gone for decades. The problem was that an overwhelming majority of rip drive manufacturing, a delicate and laborious affair, occurred in Terran space. 98.76824 percent, in fact. A number that Auckland knew down to the last decimal. Something that he privately took steps to maintain and push ever higher.

Of course the council had to watch. The factories couldn't be risked. So long as the Xen'wa didn't pose an actual threat to the factories and didn't threaten to cut off the council's supply, they were free to do as they wished. Their people needed the drives. Their economies were dependent upon them. So what if this escalated into a small border war? Afterall, the Xen'wa would be the only ones to pay the costs, the Council was free of it.

"We will have our recompense!" the Xen'wa tried once more. This was it. This was the moment. The Terrarch had given him a card to play at the correct time and Auckland could feel now was it. He couldn't help it, a malicious smile played over his face, not that the other species would recognize it.

"How's this for recompense, you daft fool. The Terrarch sends a message: 'Effective immediately: A 1000% duty on all rip drives leaving for Xen'wa space. Should any other species trade to them for less than 800, they will have the same.'"

A wave rippled through the chamber, silence following closely behind it. A few, it passed over, not touching them. Their drives went through other species' space. A few, it rankled uncomfortably. They would have to take their shipments around Xen'wa space instead of through. More jumps. A few saw opportunity, a quick way to fill their coffers. Fewer still saw it for what it was.

The faintest beginnings of an insidious threat.

Back in his personal office at the Terran embassy, Auckland leaned back in his chair. He ran his hands back and forth across the familiar arms, fingers dancing across the familiar creases in the leather, fondling the large brass rivets delicately. At last, with his thumbs rubbing circles through the lacquer on the mahogany arms, he couldn't take it any more. He reached forward, grabbing one of the hard kiwifruit-flavored candies from the bowl and popped it in his mouth. He rolled it in his mouth for a moment, taking in its taste before violently spitting it out across the room.

With forceful, angry motions, he activated his terminal and opened up a communication stream. He only had to wait a few moments before he saw that the person on the other side had joined.

Boer?

Auckland?

You best be right.

He severed the connection, breathing heavily. His eyes raced around the room, fingers tapping where his keyboard had been projected just moments before. He grabbed another piece and threw it into his mouth, biting down hard enough for it to shatter into pieces.

Damn, he hated kiwifruit.

CHAPTER FIVE

"Always be wary of the most dangerous dagger. It will not come in the form of metal, wielded by the hand of another. It will always come from within. It is the dagger that we wield ourselves that is always the most dangerous, the most potent, the most accurate. That is the dagger that will always strike true and shatter the core of yourself."

-- Wisdoms of the Terrarch

T he door hissed behind the simple screen of her secured terminal, the whirr of the dehumidifiers already spinning up and destroying the silence of Boer's chambers. Standing in the doorway, still sealed by a murky membrane designed to help lock out the humidity, was a construct. The Thlassians had produced it, a short, squat, ugly thing with several large, flexible appendages not unlike their cluster at their front. She groaned internally, suppressing a soft shudder as she remembered his appearance, the way his tentacles and arms had floated beneath him. Were she a less educated woman, her baser instinct would win over at their monstrous appearance.

She quickly closed out her terminal before standing and walking over to the machine. Her feet slipped slightly on the smooth metallic floors, the socks she wore gaining little traction on the polished metal surface. She should have thought to bring socks with a little more grip. As she walked, she took another glance at the quarters.

All said, they had done a remarkable job, closely matching the specifications that the diplomatic office had provided. To her left, a small room with a comfortable, if somewhat cramped, sleeping bunk reminiscent of what one would find on one of the diplomatic shuttles she was now accustomed to. To the right, the bathroom, complete with all the proper accommodations required by human biology. The commode was slightly cold, but certainly functional. She remembered the confusion that both species had as they were trying to explain the purpose of them. One species that releases directly into the water and the other who just let it fall when needed, being aerial. They found having something that involved one's biological waste in one's main habitat … odd.

She tread past the simple cooking features, which, while rudimentary, gleamed brightly in the artificial lights. The Ambassador had brought dozens of packets of MREs from Earth, sanitized by the vacuum that they were packed in. However, the Thlassians had still undertaken great pains in order to provide more substantial fare and comforts. She wondered where the Thlassians had procured the produce that rested in the refrigerator that sat in the corner. All in all, it was quite comfortable. She had almost called it cozy.

This, of course, was complicated by the fact that the habitat was nestled over one hundred and fifty meters under the planet's sea. The Thlassians, however, had risen to the challenge admirably. The entirety of the structure was built in a timeframe that would make even the Terran shipyards feel miffed. Despite her looking, Boer hadn't found any signs of leaks, cracks, or areas still unfinished in her short travels between her quarters and the diplomatic chamber. The entire construction seemed perfectly suited to resist the crushing force of the depths that she was now at.

What was even further impressive was that the entire thing was pressurized separately from the atmosphere. Normally, the depth would have made transitioning between the bottom and surface complicated due to accumulation of gasses in the tissues of her body. The Thlassians had, however, constructed the building so that once you entered, it sealed and maintained surface pressure throughout. This allowed Boer the freedom to visit the surface as she wished, instead of having to go through long depressurization regimes. Boer gazed at the window to the depths beyond and couldn't guess at the unimaginable force that it was holding out. The entire reason why you would pressurize a structure such as this was to help resist it.

She queued a few panels, and then the membrane retracted with a soft sucking sound that she still wasn't accustomed to. She looked out at the construct. It was largely shaped like a curved obelisk, a small dome mounted on the front. On the center of the construct, a small screen that had the dark and shadowy figure of Ambassador Gwooon. Down its sides, Boer could see the beginnings of several flexible limbs, akin to Gwooon's arms, bending back into a cluster behind it. It vaguely gave the entire construct a reflective, measured feeling to it.

"Forgive the intrusion, Ambassador Boer. I just wished to inform you that we are finished with Ambassador Stresi's orientation with the translators. It was … unpleasant." Boer let out a chuckle, still marveling at the ease at which the Thlassian translators tried to phrase it in a way that she would understand. She had anticipated a horrendously troublesome device. Instead, it had slotted quite naturally into their discourse.

"Ambassador, I do not observe the humor." His tentacles braided together into two larger masses, a faint yellow beginning to flicker over them. Boer wondered at the gesture and colorations. Confusion? Uncertainty?

"I'm sorry," BOO-BOOP. "Translator - Add: Sorry - A feeling of distress that is usually caused by a shared pain. Gwooon, I was simply observing the quality of your translators. They truly are remarkable devices."

She motioned the construct inside, before walking to the

large couch that wreathed the far wall. Behind it was a large curtain, closed at the moment. Boer had found the shapes that moved through the dark, shadowed world outside the window... distressing.

She motioned for the construct to join her before flopping down onto the cushions. She picked at the small tray of reconstituted food that lay on the couch by the terminal as he approached. The constructs were a reasonable solution to the need to communicate outside of water and with a modicum of privacy, though Boer still had issues with the concept of it. Partly due to the fact that they weren't exactly fast on their feet.

When the construct arrived, jerkily rotating on the spot to once more face her with the screen, Boer saw that Gwooon had moved to a relaxed state, his limbs hanging low beneath him and off screen. "Might I inquire: Do you find the accommodations acceptable?"

"The accommodations are phenomenal," BOO-BOOP. "Translator - Add: Phenomenal - far past the expectation in an extremely positive manner. Gwooon, I appreciate all that your species has done to facilitate."

And they truly had. The Thlassians had built the entirety of the structure in the ten star dates it took to hash out all of the details and arrive. In that time, they had only made three insistences, the first of which: Boer's quarters must be housed under the ocean's surface. Looking around it, one wouldn't be able to tell the structure had been assembled so quickly. There were none of the tell-tale signs of haste and compromise in it.

"Might I inquire: could we have our first conversation now?" There was the second.

Over the course of the talks, Boer had to do just that. Talk. They claimed that it was to better train the translator, but Boer was aware of no similar stipulation being placed on the Xen'wa. Boer found that curious. Of course, there was always the option that such talks *were* occurring and the Terrans simply hadn't been informed, but Boer didn't think so. Something in her told her the truth of this. Maybe it was Ambassador Stresi's necessitated departures that had made the Thlassians not request it.

"Certainly, Gwooon. What did you want to discuss?"

The third and final stipulation was a data packet containing a complete lexicon of any Terran word that had a direct parallel to Galactic Standard, to be delivered upon the arrival of the shuttles. Undoubtedly, Gwooon would already have this, though Boer imagined he hadn't the time to actually look at any of it.

"Your choice. The topic does not matter," he intoned softly.

Boer thought for a moment. There was so much: histories, foods, customs, countries, ideologies. She hadn't the faintest idea of where to begin. An idea flooded its way quickly through Boer's mind. A way to get a measure of him.

"I'm sorry, Gwooon, I wouldn't know where to begin. You decide."

Gwooon floated gently on the screen. The only motion he made was to bundle his appendages underneath himself once more. His skin, however, *that* was of great interest to Boer. It started on the edges of his frill, but slowly worked its way around it until spreading to his main body. There, it deepened, darkened, and continued to overtake him, until nothing was left. Gwooon was now glowing in his entirety a deep royal blue, so dark it had almost given away to black. It was breathtaking in its clarity. Boer sat there wondering why his color had shifted so profoundly, her mind flicking to An's report once more. He had postulated that the colors correlated to emotions. At last, Gwooon spoke, the color immediately dissipating back to his natural hues.

"Might I inquire: Your planet has oceans, does it not?"

Boer's eyes went distant. She had been a fool. The damage was done, however. She should have tried to steer him elsewhere. It had been foolish of her to let him dictate where the conversation would go. There was too much danger down certain paths. She shouldn't have let him decide the direction the conversation went. Of course he would be interested in Earth's oceans, the most dangerous path of them all. Should she try to steer him elsewhere? No, that would be worse.

Nervously, she replied, her voice quiet with the weight of humanity's past.

"We did."

She looked up to Gwooon's form. It floated there, unmoving. Boer almost wanted to say judgmentally, but it somehow wasn't. She saw no reaction to it. Maybe the implication wasn't received? As the silence stretched on, she knew that wasn't it. He understood the implication perfectly. He must have. Still the silence grew, until Boer couldn't take it anymore. She had to fill it.

"Our path into the stars wasn't a gentle one. We developed far too quickly for our own good," she finally said, her eyes grown distant with hands clasped in her lap.

"In our rush forwards, a great many things came with it. War, strife, pain, pollution." BOO-BOOP. "The accumulation of unwanted and harmful chemicals and objects," she said. She struggled to find the words. "It ... harmed our oceans. We were unable to fix them. We watched as the oceans died, slowly, around us." She took a deep swallow. "We tried, you must understand. We tried so desperately hard. But by the time we *saw*, it was too late. Nothing worked. All we could do was watch as it all was lost. Slowly, our oceans died around us until there was nothing left. This led to one of the darkest times in our history. A time of monumental calamity. They are still there, monuments to what we have lost due to our foolishness, but they are great voids of life now. Whole generations have grown up with no understanding of what was lost, but they bear the scar regardless."

"Might I inquire: Your Terrarch did not see this?"

Boer let out a soft exhale. "The Terrarch was a child when all of this happened. She didn't have the means to do anything about it, no matter if she had seen it or not. She was forced to live through it."

46

"Might I inquire: When did this happen?"

"Gwooon, it was a long time ago. It is very..." she paused, thinking on the word she wanted to use to regain control of the dialog. "...difficult to talk about. I..."

For the first time since they had met, Gwooon cut her off. "I do not intend to cause distress. We will talk another time." Boer tried to say something. She felt that she was obligated to. As the construct abruptly turned, Boer even went so far as to raise one arm to stop it but then softly lowered it into her lap. The ever faint buzzing of her implants quieted.

It was their right to judge them.

One hundred and ninety-nine Thlassians were gathered to receive the data packets. They would immediately be integrated into the translators upon their arrival, to better facilitate the talks.

The Xen'wa packet was the first to arrive. The Thlassians had no issue with receiving it. It was a small thing, quickly integrated.

However, when the Terran packet arrived, the terminals beeped out an error. The file was too large. Perplexed, the Thlassians added more data storage. Again, the terminal beeped, the file was too large. Now thoroughly confused, the Thlassians again added more storage. Again, the terminal beeped, the file was too large. They began to converse, to try and find a consensus. After a time, their final member joined them, free of his duties for the day.

They tried everything they could think of. Maybe there was a corruption of some kind? Maybe the Terrans had sent the wrong format? Most dangerous of all, maybe the Terrans never intended to give it!? All of these thoughts and more were voiced. Eventually, they reached their consensus.

They would add more storage.

By the time they were done, the Thlassians finally had enough so that the terminal wouldn't beep at them.

The transfer began.

When it was done, they fed it into the translator. As they watched the data scroll by, the Terrans had, in fact, sent the requested lexicon.

But then something else scrolled by.

Most of it was indecipherable to the translator, formatted in the Terran language; it could only decipher bits and pieces that they already had the context for. When it reached its end, it began its second pass and was able to process a little bit more. Again and again, the context slowly built until the file was complete.

Unknown to Boer, The Terrarch had sent them a message.

It contained all the triumphs of the human species. All of the achievements and successes. The wonders and splendors. The great loves and joys. Moments of such beauty and light to cause tears of happiness to rain down.

Every great moment in humanity's past, she had sent.

But that was not all.

She had also sent the failures. The wars. The brutality. The violence. The sins. She sent all of the depths of depravity and shame to which humanity had gone before, and could go again. She had sent the very darkness found at the center of humanity.

She had sent everything. She held nothing back. They had it all.

They wouldn't know it at first. That would take time and patience. Just because it was translated didn't remove the need to actually spend time with it.

Deep under the waters of Thlassia, the Terrarch gave every piece of humanity to them.

And so they began.

CHAPTER SIX

"Duty should always be to the forefront. What can you do? Not for yourself, but for those around you. What can you do? Can you help? Can you empower? Can you aid? The universe is cruel, heartless, and yet at the core of its nature exists an uncut jewel, its surface littered with the scars of those few who tried. What will you do to bring it to its polished finish?"

-- Wisdoms of the Terrarch

An laid on his back, the thin padding barely helping to break the firm line of the concrete slab that stretched beneath him. His cell was small. A simple concrete slab with the barest of paddings, a tiny window, measuring no more than a square foot in size, a metal sink and toilet in the corner. That was it.

That was his life now. After everything that he had done, the places he had been, the cultures he had explored, it all came down to this tiny cell.

He wasn't sure how long the Terrarch intended to keep him here. It had already been ten days. An had no doubt in his mind that this was the Terrarch's doing. Who else had the power to, in one fell swoop, void his credentials, sever his tenure and fire him from the university, seize all of his cultural property for 'future return to home worlds', and then arrest him and bring him here. No, this had to be her.

It was the why of it that he couldn't understand. He had always served faithfully, and the Terrarch encouraged well voiced dissent, provided it was reasoned and carefully done. The Terrarch wouldn't have taken such a drastic action to one who had been so useful as he. His past had guaranteed her support.

No, this had to be Boer. Boer was the reason he was here. He thought of the night before when he had plunged into the depths of despair that the plan had thrust him. A revelation came to An. While the Terrarch might appreciate reasoned discourse, she didn't want it distracting Boer.

That's it, then. An resigned himself to the dark times ahead. The Terrarch would keep him here until it was all done. There was no other option, of course. The Terrarch saw that. She had seen through him, seen the despair that the idea of this course had brought to An, and had known that it would have consumed him fully. He thought about what he might have done, might still do if he was let out. An shuddered.

No, she was right to do this. If she hadn't, he might have already actively worked against Boer. As dark as the future could be, there was a ray of light in it all. If Boer was able to successfully pull it all off, then there might just be a future for all parties involved at the end of it. An prayed that she was somehow successful, though a large part of him wished she wouldn't be. It would be better for the stability of most if she failed, even if it doomed humanity.

He continued to lay there like this, caught in the split that he carried within his own mind, when the door opened and the guards ordered him to stand. Somewhat forcefully, he was led through the facility until the walls gave way from their stark, brutalist design and moved over to darker blacks, well polished and gleaming.

An had thought that he was in a jail. It became clear to him now that this wasn't the case. The facility that he was passing through wasn't designed for detention. Instead, An could see that it was set to a purpose. Onwards through the facility they went, eventually passing doorways that led to neat rows of cubicles, each with someone hard at work, analyzing and monitoring the various data streams that were coming into the building. Eventually, he was led to a large chamber set in the center of the building. There he saw it.

On the far wall, a display. It was currently streaming a live view of a Xen'wa. An stilled as he realized it was Ambassador Stresi, all puffed up in the throes of aggression. He was sitting on his roost, dyed in a dazzling display of color that made him look as though he were made of fire. The colors made sense, given the context. Of course Ambassador Stresi would have settled on the orange of anger and the red of superiority.

It's today, An realized with a start. The first day of negotiations. Judging by what was being displayed on the screens, An could tell it was going poorly. Extremely poorly.

Stresi's crest was fully erect, standing proud and tall over the top of his head as it weaved back and forth in the motions of dismissal. He watched as the talons on Stresi's feet opened and closed, shuffling in a way that indicated annoyance. Occasionally, he would circle his wings, great massive things that would usually be tucked behind, before him, flexing the small talons that rested at the end of them, indicating open hostility and arrogance. In this stance, he resembled some great warrior puffing up his chest. Unbidden, he had a thought of Auckland, in the middle of a great Haka that his people were performing for the Terrarch. On the right corner of the screen, An could see the curve of a nose.

"As I said, we still need him," came the Terrarch's voice from the corner of the room. Startled, An turned. She was seated on a simple stool, her back resting against the wall. She had been watching him, observing him as he took in Stresi's form.

"In twenty seconds, he saw more of the situation than you have in the past ten minutes."

Around her stood two of An's colleagues, each the pinnacle of their individual fields. With the three of them together, it represented a gathering of the three greatest minds in the study of other species. Xenobiology, the study of their unique bodies and how they function on a biological level. Xenolinguistics, a study of their actual languages and how their usage impacts and influences meaning. And finally An, representing Xenology, the study of the whole creature, their culture, their passions and drives.

He wasn't being punished. He was being sent a message. The Terrarch's message said two things:

First, humanity was fully invested. Everything that humanity had was focused towards this plan.

Second, there will be no undermining Boer's focus.

He understood.

"Very well. Thank you for this informative session. Now the Terran Federation knows our next steps," the human ambassador said, tapping the small stack of what she called *paper*, a fibrous accumulation of organics native to the Terran homeworld, on the surface of the table. Throughout the entirety of the meeting, she had been scribing something onto the surface. Notes, it seemed. Stresi scoffed at how feeble her mind must be that she couldn't follow something as simple as this. She carefully placed them in the small contraption she had carried in with her, the top of which closed with two loud clicking noises.

"I bid you both clear skies and calm waters," she said, nodding to each as she gave the cultural farewells of both ambassadors.

As she departed, the false hooves she wore clicking against the steel floor, Ambassador Stresi shuffled on his roost. He was simultaneously pleased and annoyed at her sharp departure. This entire process was proving to be as much of a waste as he had thought.

Once the door closed behind her, Stresi let out a soft trill which Ambassador Gwooon was beginning to believe conveyed an emotion akin to smugness. Stresi followed it up with a series of clicks and trills which the translator device took a moment to process before it released the deep echoes into Gwoon's tank.

"Looks like the war will continue then. She shows her fear plainly."

Stresi preened, proud of himself. However, when no message came from his colleague, he turned his head. In his tank, Gwooon's limbs were motionless, but his skin was flashing dozens of colors as he floated in the tank. The colors were a dazzling display that covered the full spectrum for Stresi, though there were chunks missing here and there, undoubtably colors that he hadn't evolved to see. He had never seen such a display from a Thlassian. What little interactions that the Xen'wa had with their species had always given the impression that they were a very calm and measured species. He had trouble reconciling his notions with the display that was occurring before him.

A few faint chirps, "Have you taken ill?"

Slowly, the colors settled, ending on a blue that closely matched the natural color of the water in the Thlassian's tank. He floated like that, motionless, nearly invisible in the water, before letting out the haunting echoes that comprised his language.

"Pleased with yourself, are you?"

"Naturally. I made her show weakness. I thank you for providing the impartial grounds for these negotiations. It allowed us to see the way to rise in this war." Gwooon continued to float motionlessly, the mass of appendages that served as his "front" facing towards where the human ambassador had departed. "She fled the negotiations, so too will her species flee from the war."

"You are such a BOO-BOOP." Stresi was momentarily caught off guard by the chime of the translator, indicating an untranslatable word. He was about to question it, when ambassador Gwooon continued on.

"Forgive me. Translator: Add word, Wooawiah - A foolish

parasitic worm found in the depths of the ocean." Stresi waited. "Known for attaching to the bottom of other creatures in an attempt to hijack their biological functions. However, frequently, they misattach to creatures that take advantage of their imperatives to efficiently harvest them for food, leading to death."

The Xen'wa ambassador stilled, considering the implications. After a moment, he discarded the thoughts. He understood what the Terrans were. Weaklings at heart. Their insistence on these very negotiations proved that. They would do anything to avoid conflict, even debasing themselves in front of this lesser species. Weaker still were the Thlassians. They didn't even have a fleet worth tracking. Stresi despised being here, but he had been ordered by his Queen to pursue this avenue. Perhaps it would resolve things quicker.

After a moment, Gwooon pressed on. "Tell me, what is it that you should fear most about the Terrans?"

"Fear? Why should we fear them? Yes, they have a sizable star fleet, replete with atomics. However, they tend towards diplomacy. While they have been able to provide a small difficulty for our fleet, you cannot deny that we hold a respectable number of their world-nests already. We hold the position of power in the negotiations. It's only sensible that all accommodation should be done on their end. We demand our recompense." A single line of red shimmered down the Thlassian.

"..."

"Should they be respected as a worthy adversary? Certainly. But fear? No more than any other near-equal. In addition, their territory holdings barely put them in the upper half of the known races in terms of scope, their fleet size not much better. I fail to see how we should be fearful of them beyond the normal expectations of war, Ambassador Gwooon."

"It is not the statistics that should make you fear them. It is a word they have, a concept. 'BOO-BOOP.' Translator: Relay Word Exact - *Honor*." The Xen'wa ambassador shifted on his roost, waiting for the Thalassian ambassador to get to his point.

"You see, we know the Terrans as the negotiators of the universe. They have always preferred dialogue and other options before violence. This is perhaps a product of their place in their ecology. The humans are neither of the extremes of the prey-predator hierarchy. They are the rare example of something that takes the middle road. Most of the creatures of their world are smaller than them, however, in almost all environments, there is a predatory species that is simultaneously larger and faster than them. We have become aware of some things. They have fought brutal wars, wars that have left millions of their own kind dead and buried, and yet their maps, as they call them, barely changed. They have bathed their world so thoroughly in blood that it might as well have been another ocean. And yet, throughout all of this, there exists that which should give you pause. Honor."

On his roost, the Xen'wa ambassador had stilled, his feathers flat along his back, flayed outwards in faint annoyance, but he was listening.

"A human will go into battle, risk their very lives towards some intangible gain that they have been assured exists. They will permanently maim themselves, reaching deep into impossibly hot waters, trying to pull another from danger. They set all of their best weapons aside, deeming them too cruel, too devastating, too ... Translator: Relay Words Exact: *Dishonorable*. Tends towards diplomacy, you say? No, you foolish skyborn. You just gave them a reason to discard their rules."

When the conversation finally finished, Boer's attention snapped back and she saw what she had done. She cursed, turning off the stove. When she had arrived back at the suite, her stomach had growled. She had been trying something creative to try and spice up the food. Instead, she had made what amounted to little more than a smoke bomb. She worked her way through the small apartment until she got to the main terminal to activate the ventilation fans to clear out the smoke. Once it was clear and she could see again without her eyes watering, she looked down at her food.

Oh, well, she thought to herself, dumping the remains onto a plate. She rinsed out the pan, setting it upon the stove for later use before picking the plate back up and heading over to the couch.

Fortunately, the Thlassians had seen fit to include a table that could slide out from the wall, something the Terrans *hadn't* thought to include in the designs for the suite. She had spent the first few days alternating between eating standing up and seated on the couch with the plate in her lap. Either way, she had noticed the thin seam in the wall when she came in from the negotiations. Curious, she had pressed on the wall there, worried if it was a crack, when the table slowly revealed itself. She wasn't entirely sure that it had been there the entire time. She hadn't looked closely enough.

She sat down behind the travesty that was her food, but found that she had no appetite for it. Only a small part of it was the condition of the meal. *The negotiations*, she thought to herself. They weighed heavily on her.

They were at the cusp of it all. After tonight, there would be no going back. The decisions had been made and they were now set along it. Whatever came, no matter what unintended ripples she caused, now was when they would begin to spread. She idly pushed the charred remains on her plate around, unwilling to start.

The door beeped and she leapt up, abandoning the calamitous meal that she had made. She quickly made her way to the door and queued the panels to open it. As expected, the construct that Gwooon used rested outside. Without saying a word, she stepped aside and let it pass.

Despite her misgivings about the first meeting, Gwooon had surprised her. In the three days before negotiations formally started, she continued to receive his visits. She had thought that he would abandon them for the horrors of their past, yet he continued to come and converse. They spent many long hours this way. Each night, Gwooon chose the topic. He had avoided anything to do with the oceans after the first night, instead diving deep into Terran culture. Boer suspected that the Terrarch had done something to steer their focus, but had no way of verifying, short of out outright asking her.

They had spent the entire third night discussing the great authors of humanity's past, Shakespeare and Voltaire. Machiavelli and Dickens. Tolstoy and Dostoevsky. She even shared thoughts on Murakami and Lu Xun. On and on their conversation flowed, consuming the time away into the depths of night. Boer had asked him that night why he had come back. He floated silently for a while, his colorations taking on that strange blue tint again. Finally, he had simply replied that he required context. Boer had spent a long time pondering that reply as she lay in bed that night.

When the construct had reached the couch, it paused before extending one of its arms to point down at the burnt and charred pile of mush that sat on Boer's plate.

"Might I inquire: Is this what your species calls food?" he said simply.

Flushed, Boer started to reply when it was riven from her body by a realization. "Gwooon!" she cried. "Did you just tell a joke?"

She watched as the construct turned, revealing Gwooon. On the small screen, his frill was flapping wildly. He had turned a deep shade of green. Realizing that this must be some display of humor, Boer began to laugh, a great deep thing that shook its way through her body. She had to put one hand on her belly before it would finally calm.

They began their conversation for the night. It continued far longer than Boer had intended, taking up most of the night as their dialog twisted and turned through the histories of the great orators of the past. Eventually, the conversation took a turn to the next day.

"I'm afraid that Ambassador Stresi has informed us he will not be coming down in the morning. I am unsure if he will be staying for further talks."

A soft smile played on Boer's face, a glint of something a little bit … savage… playing across her eyes before she quelled it back down to her depths.

"Don't worry Gwooon, I am sure that he will be joining us later in the day." She leaned back into the cushions, her head resting on the small lip of the window. Her hair brushed against the soft curtain.

"Might I inquire?" he said cautiously. Boer thought for a good long while. She half-expected Gwooon to question her again, but his patience let the silence between them stretch. Eventually, Boer broke it.

"I fear that the Defense Fleet will introduce them to another human concept. I do not know if the Xen'wa will be able to process the concept adequately or not. I will admit, its uncertainty has me nervous." Her eyes went distant as she thought of the repercussions. If this was not interpreted by the Xen'wa correctly, then the whole thing would come crumbling down at the beginning. It also depended heavily on Auckland and Fletcher to perform their roles.

"You speak as though you do not have authority?"

"I remind you, our definitions vary slightly for the word 'Ambassador.' Your people, as well as the Xen'wa, use the term to signal someone who speaks *for* your species. Someone that has been granted the right to settle things completely and that the rest of the species will be bound by it, a thing of great trust." She paused for a moment, wondering if the translator would understand the inflection. It didn't beep. "For the humans, an ambassador is someone who has the authority to *represent*. Any agreements that come have to be filtered to the individual who actually speaks for the species. The Terrarch. It is she who decides. We informed both of you about this before talks began.

"In your culture, the role of the Ambassador is almost

absolute. You give away the full authority of your leadership to your Ambassadors so that they may make the binding agreement at the moment. Humanity is a more measured thing." She held up her hand. "I do not mean to imply that it is better in some way, simply that there is a difference."

Gwooon started another long silence. This one Boer had no intention of breaking, picking once more at her food. They sat like that, occasionally Boer noticed a flicking motion of Gwooon's arms, mostly shielded by his larger tentacles. She suspected that Gwooon was communicating with another, using a language that they had not programmed the translators to pick up. She had known that this could be a possibility.

After five minutes of silence between them, the construct turned to depart. Boer called out a question that had been bothering her. When she had received the briefing packet, no mention had been made to any flecking on their skin. Boer was curious as to its meaning. It was probably just a slight genetic mutation, but she desperately wanted to know.

"May I inquire:" she started, trying out the phrase that Gwooon started most of his questions with. The construct turned to her, so she continued on. "I noticed that you have some permanent discoloration on your body. I was curious as to its reason," she said neutrally.

A soft green flicked through his body. It wasn't nearly as all encompassing as the blue that Boer had seen the other day, just enough to cause a noticeable tint to him. Were he human, she might have assumed that he was sick. One of his arms wrapped around his body and rubbed at one of the green flecks on his skin.

"It is a marking of the life I have lived, remnants of the past." He didn't elaborate, he just turned and continued on. When the construct reached the thin line of where the membrane would extend, it paused, turning once more to face her. "Might I inquire?"

"Certainly, Gwooon."

"Could you tell me exactly what *is* this concept that the

fleet might introduce to them?"

"It might be hard for you to understand. It is based on something that would be foreign to you, being an ocean dwelling species."

Gwooon stood there in silence. Boer had learned that this was a quirk of their species. When something didn't need to be said, they often just didn't, deferring to silence. Boer found this trait most uncomfortable. There was a certain gravity to it.

"We call it 'Scorched Earth.'"

Later, looking down at her plate, she realized she didn't know what to do with the food. There wasn't a trash receptacle. She certainly didn't want it in her body.

Eventually, she just picked it up and walked over to the toilet.

"Begin rip," intoned the firm voice of the Admiral.

Immediately, all around him throughout Command, the crew of the *Destiny* began their work, ensuring that all readings and data streams with the Crocketts were synced. Energy began working its way down through the massive relays and worked its way into the spherical rip drive that sat in its shielded compartment. Slowly, their drive spooled up, gathering the great gravitational wave that would rip and tear its way through space.

"Coordinates locked."

"Readings nominal."

Admiral Fletcher looked around the bridge at his crew as they worked with the utmost efficiency. Each had been hand selected by either himself or Vice Admiral Coeur, and each were experts in their respective fields. Assisted by the defensive AI that the ship housed, the drive was expertly cared for and maintained, flawlessly performing its job.

Of course, their drive was tuned differently from most drives in the galaxy. As it spooled up, a second gravitational wave also spooled, the opposite of its predecessor. When they both released, yes, the rip would still happen and fling them through the stars. However, when they released the second wave, it would be the perfect opposite to the first. Nullifying it. They couldn't mask their departure if someone was looking, they would detect the initial spool up even if they stopped the wave from rippling outwards. However, they did still have one great benefit to this added effort.

They would arrive, silently.

It was the epitome of rip drive technology, something the Terrans wisely kept to themselves. They understood the implications of it. The galaxy at large was not yet ready for something of this magnitude, the ability to silently arrive wherever they chose. Fletcher harbored sincere doubts as to whether they ever would be. No, the Terrans had elected to keep this to themselves. Most of the ships of the Terran Defense Fleet already had the technology. What few ships didn't were being retrofitted even now in the Mars shipyards. They would all be ready in time. Barely, but they would. The only way to detect where the Terran Defense Fleet was would be an unfortunate rip directly onto a satellite.

He steeled himself. This was it, the final rip. Afterwards, the *Destiny* would be in position for each of its missions. With this he would be poised to deliver the deadly cargo that he had carried all the way from the Sol system. He would be ready to fully enact Boer's plan. All he would have to do is await the order.

"Commence final rip."

Immediately, the deck beneath his feet shook with force as the galaxy tore itself apart. Massive waves of gravity lurched out from the ship, distorting and bending the view screen. They went completely black when the second wave was also fired, completing the initial rip. Slowly, the rattling of the bridge intensified. On the view screens, the galaxy began to put itself back together, a mosaic of waves and colors as the localized distortion from their arrival petered out. When it all stopped, Admiral Fletcher gave the call out. "Coordinates?"

"Coordinates are good. Rip was successful."

"Very good. Vice-Admiral Coeur, you have command."

"I have Command," she replied.

In his quarters, Admiral Fletcher sat at his terminal. He had been sitting there for the past ten minutes, slowly opening and closing his hands. The report to the Terrarch had come easily. It was his duty and like always, he fulfilled it fully. This though … for this he had trouble finding the words.

Eventually deciding to just take the plunge, he queued the communication function up and waited for the other to join. Eventually, she did.

Boer?

Yes?

Fletcher sat there. He didn't know what to say. A simple "In position" would suffice. Hell, even just typing "Here" would do. All he could do, however, was stare at that blinking vertical line that kept flashing before his eyes. His hands would not move. He tried to will them. Force them to do his bidding and type out a message, a single letter! They wouldn't.

He sat like that for a while, trying to figure out some way to let Boer know, but despite his efforts, he couldn't tame himself. Eventually, he looked up at the terminal and saw that he didn't need to. Displayed on it was a second message.

Roger.

The connection had been severed from the other end.

Without so much as a word exchanged between them, Boer had understood.

Silently, Fletcher turned his terminal off and laid down in his bed. Sleep did not come easily. His mind resisted the idea of it, images of planets flashing through. Eventually, he gave up on it and went to engineering to oversee the re-tuning of the rip drives to their second configuration.

CHAPTER SEVEN

"It is natural to fear. To Doubt. To allow the desperation of one's indecision to well up and threaten to overtake yourself. Make yourself not a vessel. Be instead the lighthouse. Fuel it with your hopes and dreams. Use your light to guide others into their own, so that when they climb the stairs, their light may continue to shine for others."

-- Wisdoms of the Terrarch

With a soft beep that pierced through the darkened chamber, the terminal pulled Fletcher back to awareness. Groggily, he shook himself awake, the lights already responding to his movement. A sharp knock sounded twice on the door to his stateroom, before opening, revealing Vice-Admiral Coeur, already mid-salute. The Admiral waved her off with a quick salute of his own, the sleep causing the room to be unfocused and blurry.

"Five minutes, Sir," she said, before making her way to the conference room. The door hissed closed. Fletcher sat on the edge of the bed for a moment, his hands exploring the small crease where his mattress met the frame. With a deep sigh, he pushed himself to his feet.

He quickly dressed himself before grabbing a cup of coffee from beside the waiting urn. When the AI detected that he was awakening, it had already brewed a fresh pot for him and filled a cup. It now sat steaming on the edge of his desk, likely the only comfort he would find today. He wrapped his hand around the small cup and opened his door. Stepping out into the hall, he quickly saluted his way through the arteries of the ship before reaching *Destiny's* core.

In Command, forty officers were working on their terminals. Occasionally, he could catch a few of them shooting nervous glances in his direction, but most were staying focused on the task. Fletcher dreaded what this meeting would mean, but also understood its importance. He looked out at his crew, taking them in as they worked their terminals, before making his way to the conference room that sat at the back, behind soundproof walls.

The frail form of the Terrarch already dominated the screen. Fletcher could see that she was in a hospital bed, dark blue marks encircling her body, wrapping around the dozens of ports that she had for direct-feed medicines. Fletcher quickly snapped to attention before being released by the shaky return of the Terrarch.

"I'm not going to bandy about, Admiral. Operation Gáe Bulg is authorized. Set to commence at 2050 Earth Time. Earth out." As she finished, her elderly form disappeared, the screen switching back to its standard clock display. A moment later and the time shimmered from 1856 to 1847 as the time packet arrived, an elegant solution to the small dilation that the ship experienced. *Two hours*, he thought to himself, before turning.

Stepping back on the bridge proper, he could already see his men getting to it as the orders flashed their screens. The mood of the bridge had changed. Where they had been cheery and anticipating the journey ahead, they had reached the moment of turbulent waters. Each had come to terms with what they must do. Each bore the weight in their own way.

The TSS Destiny's Spear was a marvel of human ingenuity. Comprising a full year's supply of minerals from the Kuiper Belt, the massive flagship of the Terran Defense Fleet stretched for a mile at its longest. Every square inch of the hull was dedicated to batteries and defenses, all nestled neatly in armor plating that could be measured by the yard. It had been designed as a defensive vessel first and foremost. The most dangerous part of it was not the weaponry that it bore on its skin, but the fleet that it carried within.

As it floated in the deep space between the stars, the five smaller unmanned ships, each a testament to a side of humanity's engineering in their own right, began to spool up their engines. At 2050, the first of the Crocketts disappeared into the inky black. A few hours later, each moment carefully calculated, recalculated, and then double checked once more, the remaining ships also vanished, leaving the Destiny alone in the dark, its monstrous wards gone.

So it is done, Admiral Fletcher thought to himself, his expression somber. He took off his hat and placed it on the command station before turning and facing the officers. He was met by equally grim faces.

He sighed deeply, before starting. "What we do today will be a burden that we each must find a way to carry. It is something that we will have to wrestle with in the dark of night. Know that what we do, we do for the sake of humanity, for the sake of the galaxy. While this will haunt each and everyone of us, know that it is in the pursuit of safeguarding the peace. Since we took to the stars, our soft words have served as our shield, but the time of soft words has failed. What we do now, we do because we must. Our foes have deafened themselves to the softness of discourse. Now is the time of the stick." He paused for a moment. That was all he had prepared, but looking at Vice-Admiral Coeur, he felt that he should say something more, something demanded it.

"Know that while it was your fingers that struck the keys, this is not yours to bear. I alone should bear this sin. Rest well. You have done your duty." As one, the officers of the bridge saluted him. He almost didn't have the heart to return it.

When he returned to his quarters, he opened up the feed to Satellite Gliese 667 C Theta. He stared silently as a small countdown displaying the remaining hours appeared in the bottom right corner, undoubtedly added by the support AI.

On the screen, a small planet flashed. Fletcher knew that the size betrayed the truth, as he quickly adjusted the screen to fully focus on the planet. Fletcher also knew what the screen didn't show. The beautiful sunrises and sunsets that blazed across the sky from the red dwarf that sat in the center of the system. The calmness of the world. The rolling oceans that humanity had spent generations seeding onto the planet. When thoughts of his upcoming retirement crossed his mind, it had often been filled with the calm of a planet like Gliese Prime, perhaps with someone by his side. He wondered how history would judge him for today. Maybe he would just be a dark footnote in the Terrarch's story. Hopefully, his name would be forgotten all together.

When Fletcher went and sat on his bed, a soft knock sounded on his door. He gave the motion for the AI that monitored the room to allow entry.

Vice-Admiral Coeur stood there. Her shoulders were slumped and her eyes heavy. She held one arm with the other, crossed over her midsection.

"Sir. I…" she didn't finish. Fletcher just looked up at her, taking in the burden she carried. He slid over, tapping on the spot he had once occupied with a hand.

Quietly, she walked over. Fletcher could see the strain of it all in the way that she kept her head turned downwards. The gravity of it had pulled her normally proud shoulders down.

She sat down on the bed beside him, and they both turned to watch the planet on the monitor in silence.

Fletcher made a quick motion towards the terminal and three more appeared.

CHAPTER EIGHT

"Why do you cry? Did the ground destroy you? Is that wound on your knee fatal? Is your only hope going forward to perish? Turn to the ground and say thank you. It showed you where you were weak and imparted a lesson. In time, that lesson will harden, and you will be forever marked as having learned it. It will become a part of you, something you can reflect upon the next time the ground threatens you. The ground has told you that it is there, and it is firm. Be firmer."

-- Wisdoms of the Terrarch

The door leading into the diplomatic chamber hissed open. Ambassador Boer quickly made her way to the table, heels clicking sharply on the metal floor. In the room, Ambassador Stresi's roost stood empty. Boer could see the shadowed form of Gwooon drifting silently in his tank before a light flicked on.

"Ambassador Boer. Forgive me, but Ambassador Stresi is, in fact, leaving. I left a message on the construct outside your room."

Boer had noticed the blinking light on the motionless Construct. She had, in fact, gotten the message but had chosen to proceed regardless. The possibilities and avenues this could take warranted her presence in the chamber today.

"It is of no matter, Ambassador Gwooon. I have full faith

that Ambassador Stresi will be joining us today." She quickly took her seat, unlocking the briefcase she carried, once more setting her papers neatly out in front of her.

She was meticulous with them, taking care to perfectly line up the sheets, a small habit she had since childhood, her way of controlling this small thing in her life. Her hands ruffled through the stacks, encouraging any errant corners to fall back in line. Out of the corner of her eye, she was paying close attention to Gwooon. He had once more moved his large tentacles to the forefront, blocking vision of the smaller arms. Interestingly, whereas the day before he had been a dazzle of colors that Boer had started to associate with emotions, now he was a muted dull gray.

"Might I inquire: Why would you assume such?"

Boer fiddled with one stubborn stack before becoming content with their alignment. Leaning back in the chair, she turned to face Gwooon directly.

"The Terrarch sent a message to them." The tips of Gwoon's tentacles twitched in sync with one another, a tiny motion, paired with the faintest yellow of light. Boer was sure that the motion was involuntary. She filed it away in the back of her mind. Later, she would think back to some of the other times that particular gesture had come up and see if there was any correlation that she could draw.

"Though it might take him some time to digest it," she added.

"Might I inquire: Digest? As in food?"

She laughed inwardly. "No, not as in food. Translator - Add Alternate: Digest - to take within oneself." She turned back to her papers. She was able to get through the entirety of her notes, taken after the fact of course, about her first encounter with Gwooon, before he spoke once more.

"We were unaware that the Terrans had such capabilities. If I might inquire: Why did you defer to using our translators if you already possessed one capable? Why come to us at all?"

It was a fair question, though Boer didn't want to get into

an in depth conversation on the topic of semiotics. Too much specialized language would have to be added to their translators in order to fully flesh out that topic. She let out a deep sigh before her eyes became distant and firm.

"Some messages need no translation." She turned back to her papers once more. Her eyes remained unfocused, staring at something that lay far past the papers that rested before her. "Certain things are universal."

She saw a deep blue glow overtake Gwooon. That glow had happened a few times before, and she began flicking through her notes as she checked for other instances. She was on the third sheet when Gwooon's translator sounded again.

"I spent a large portion of the break thinking about that concept you mentioned. 'Scorched Earth'."

She turned back to him. Over the past few days, Boer had grown accustomed to the flashing of colors that danced across his skin, this time, various swirls and mixtures of blues. At times, she found them quite beautiful, reminiscent of the dazzling displays out amongst the stars. They held a gravity to them that she felt affecting her. Even now, Gwooon was still consumed by a slight blue hue. It rippled and spiraled across his skin in a hypnotic display.

"I have pondered on several such meanings that could be derived from this phrase, yet I find myself caught in the trappings of why? Might I inquire: Why is your planet scorched? Is it in reference to some natural disaster in the past of your planet?"

"No, Ambassador Gwooon, it is not," She said firmly, hesitating if she should continue on. She weighed her responsibilities, and settled on the realization that the damage was already done. Distressed as she was about the events that were playing out, and the course that would be set as a result of them, she had misspoke.

She should have never mentioned the concept to Gwooon.

"You see, the word Earth is not only used to refer to the planet, but also the ground of the planet. When we refer to the concept of scorched earth, it is primarily a military doctrine, though some apply it to other aspects of life as well. The general idea of it is to provide no aid, comfort, respite, or succor to one's enemies. Should your enemies be advancing into your crops, burn them. Should they be entering into your cities, level them. Show the enemy that the only advance can be through a barren wasteland. Inform them that this barrenness will be the only prize from war."

Gwooon went motionless in the tank, the blue darkening until he was stained by it, streaks of yellow occasionally cut through. Boer had come to realize this was something that he often did when in thought, though the addition of yellow was a surprise.

"You see, that is what we call 'digesting an idea'," she said softly, pointing to the tank. He dipped his front slightly.

"Might I inquire: How would one apply that to space?"

"It's simple really, brutally so. You take away the things that your enemy wants and needs. You deny him his objectives, remove those pieces from the board. You make it so that anything, any movement, be it forward, retreat, or anything lateral, comes at an exorbitant cost for all involved. This war started on a simple premise. The idea that they could take a planet. We understand several core things about this task of theirs. First, the ships in question were not their most modern nor most powerful. Nor were they fitted with ripdrives. This means that the only way they could have reached our systems were sublight drives, implying that this was something that they started at least fifty cycles ago. That is where their closest system to ours is. They elected to only bring the minimum amount they thought they needed to take their target.

"This was an intentional, planned thing. We were willing to chalk that up to testing the waters so to say," BOO-BOOP "Translator: Add phrase: Testing the waters - Trying to ascertain a situation through a trial of some kind with no actual commitment.

"However, over the past four weeks, I apologize, twenty

two star dates, it has become abundantly clear that the Xen'wa do not see humanity as a danger. Instead, they see us as prey, something they can consume at their leisure. The Terrarch sought to dissuade them of this notion. Now, I apologize, but I seek to finish preparations for the meeting."

As Boer continued to take in the papers in front of her, Gwooon watched her intently. He found the strange mannerisms of these creatures to be remarkably interesting.

Also interesting to him, however, were the quirks of genetics that his species had yet to reveal to others. His species was particularly sensitive to electromagnetic waves, however minute. It was what allowed them to advance further into the realm of sentience than the other species of their planet. They had felt the world around them alive with these waves, and their intelligence had developed as they sought to understand them.

Even separated as he was by the confines of his tank, he was not blind to the fact that Ambassador Boer gave off three such signatures: one from her left eye, another from her left ear, and the final a repeating signal coming from her chest. The third seemed to be organic, likely the process through which her species circulated blood. The first two, however, remained a mystery to him. He wanted to ask her about them, but the question seemed rude. To Gwooon's other senses, the eye seemed to be designed in a way to closely match its pair. Perhaps it was some form of prosthetic, meant to mask some deformity. Gwooon didn't wish to offend, so he remained silent.

As he watched, time ticking slowly by, he suddenly saw her ear twitch, and left eye became unfocused for but a moment. Gwooon couldn't control himself as he once more went into a deep thought, the action shining on his skin. *Perhaps she isn't truly alone...*

"Ambassador Stresi should be joining us shortly," Boer said, carefully removing the stacks of papers and returning them to her briefcase. Gwooon's communication terminal flashed a series of lights, invisible to the human that sat obliquely from his tank.

"Ambassador Stresi is descending to the landing pad. He is also requesting that he be allowed to bring in two personal guards, part of his diplomatic attachment."

Boer clicked her briefcase shut.

"If they are not armed, allow them in."

"Are you sure? Should they attack, we do not wish to be viewed as *poor hosts.*" The translator had done something odd. It had changed its intonation of the last two words. It had never done this before. Boer made a mental note. She would have to consider the implications of that later but for now, she had something far more tenuous to weave.

"It will be fine, so long as they are unarmed."

A short while later, the door on the opposite from where she entered opened, revealing the feathered forms of three Xen'wa. The first she immediately recognized was that of Ambassador Stresi. While all three of them looked physically near identical to Boer, their colorations were starkly different. Whereas Stresi was still an extravagant display of bright reds and oranges, the two guards at his flanks were muted grays, trailing to black. Boer made a mental note that these colors were likely products of dyes and that she would have to inquire to the support team their purpose, to see if they had any hidden meaning.

The two guards were dressed like Stresi. Mostly nude, with only a breastplate of some kind fashioned across their chest. Whereas Stresi's was made of some thin fabric, the two guards' gave off a metallic sheen. Their three clawed hands that rested at the end of the long arms that doubled as wings were empty. The display wasn't offensive, of course. Their avian nature left little to be offended by.

Before even taking his roost, Stresi was already unleashing a cacophony of noises that the translator struggled to keep pace with. A few notable translations were monsters, creatures, dung eaters and featherless, to name a few as the translator maintained a stream of apoplectic beeps throughout. Boer just sat still, a slight smile on her face as the Xen'wa tired himself out. At last, he settled on his roost.

"I would remind you of decorum in the future, Ambassador Stresi," came the soft voice of Gwooon's translator.

"Decorum!" Stresi screeched. "DECORUM!?!?! Do you know what these flightless dung-eaters have done?!?" Even without the translator, Boer had no issues with picking up the obvious emotion in his gestures. "Four nest-worlds, Gone!" He clicked his beak. "Just like that." He turned back to face Boer. "How many of your own kind did you just doom to fall?"

Boer's voice was quiet, barely above a whisper, completely calm and devoid of any emotion or inflection. Nothing else would have cut through the Xen'wa's anger quite so effectively.

"None."

The Xen'wa leaned dangerously far back on his perch, before catching himself.

"You speak untruthfully!" he said, his voice low and not unlike a hiss.

Boer let out another long sigh when Gwooon saw some emotion that he had never seen on her face flit into her eyes, narrowing them. Her entire demeanor had shifted, as though she were no longer the Boer that he had conversed with not moments ago, but was instead some dangerous creature poised to strike down the Xen'wa ambassador. He weighed it against all the information that he had been briefed on. Her eyes loomed large in his mind, swallowing and devouring him piece by piece. He couldn't help the slashes of yellow that worked their way across his body.

"Stresi, in this entire 'misunderstanding,' as your species likes to call it, there have only been four human casualties."

Stresi went still, his eyes focused intensely on the threat before him.

"Four workers on a satellite that you inadvertently destroyed with one of your debris shields as you flew into the system. Small odds, that. You then engaged with our local defense drones, unmanned craft, tasked with ensuring the law and order of the system.

"Yes, you did manage to destroy all two hundred and fifty of them, however, there was not a single human aboard. In the same span, you lost one hundred and thirty eight vessels of your own. Military ships. I wonder how many lives were lost in that process."

Stresi's beak had opened a little, allowing Boer to see into his toothless mouth.

"You want to measure this conflict in lives, so be it. We have lost four. What is your count at?"

She stood placidly, gathering her briefcase with calm, controlled motions.

"You wanted to go to war with the Terrans? You were desperate to find out what it would be like? Fine. Then *listen* to us as we show you."

"I say again you LIE!" he hissed back at her. Boer had been collecting a stack of paper off of the table, but moved her hand to place it out on the table and let out a low grumble. Her form softened for a moment, then quickly found its edge once more.

"Would you like to know what that small satellite was responsible for?

"Observation.

"Its role was to monitor any and all traffic coming into the system through sublight means. We detected your fleet well before you began deceleration. In the eighteen star dates before your ships entered your own sensor ranges, the planets had already been completely evacuated. There was not a soul aboard them when you arrived. Save the four souls who stayed to do their duty, the entire system was empty of life."

She paused for a moment, her voice dropping slightly.

"Terrans don't often go to war. We have learned our lesson from the past. We have spent far too much time on the brink by our own doing. We chose to exist peacefully among the stars. The Xen'wa have disturbed that. You saw a planet and planned to take it. You started this 'misunderstanding' but you also speak for your people. Yesterday, you acknowledged this for what it was."

She looked up at Stresi, eyes locking with his across the table.

"'War.'"

Gwooon stilled. Ambassador Boer had not been present for that conversation, having left moments prior.

"I would remind you, your species proffered atomics, the pinnacle of your research, as your payment into the stars. Your ultimate weapon. Your great gesture out to the species of the council. When the Terrans joined the Council, we already had them. Before we even made our first infantile steps out into the stars, we had them. Our planet was stained by their use. Would it surprise you to know we have sub-categories of atomics?"

Boer paused for a moment so the stunned creature before her could even begin to digest what she had said.

"The Terrarch sends a message, no warning, no threat. I suggest you heed it: 'Leave all of Terran Space.'"

CHAPTER NINE

"Violence is not a worthy pursuit. Do not seek it out. However, always be prepared for when it finds you. At that time, embrace it. Shroud yourself with it. Become it. Only then can you hope to scare it away."

-- Wisdoms of the Terrarch

A soft chime woke Boer from her sleep, dispelling visions of planets shattering into dust, their death throes mighty things of fire and dust. She looked around the small room groggily before clapping the back of her head against the small bulkhead that hung over the bed. She slowly twisted in the bed, one hand rubbing the small lump that was already forming under her dark brown hair. Beside her, the briefcase that contained her terminal let out another of its beeps to inform her of a message.

She took no time to dress herself, still in the tight fitting undergarments she had gone to sleep in. She made her way quickly to where her briefcase rested, opened it and removed her terminal. After she logged in, there was a single message displayed, commanded to open on its own by its sender.

Ey-Er 4. Immediately.

She let out a groan, shaking the sleep from her body before

grabbing a small gray earplug, the size of the tip of her pinky. Sitting back on the bed, she placed the plug gently into her right ear. As she laid on her back, she closed her right eye before making quick movements on her left brow and behind her left ear. She braced herself for the coming nausea.

As a result of her movements, tiny gears purred behind her eye and ear as the proper channels were aligned. She wasn't quite sure how they worked, the scientist had said something about quantum bindings, but a moment later her world reeled as she now heard herself in a room abuzz with a dozen low spoken languages. Her vision shifted from the bulkhead she had just struck, showing a sight that made her mind reel. She recognized the main chambers of the Galactic Council, host to a representative from each of the seventeen member species. She had to swallow down the bile that her body tried to force out as it struggled to make sense of the fact that her left eye was now transmitting perspective from the right side of her face.

No, not her face.

Though she couldn't look down at it, having no control over the eye, she caught the slightest curve of a cheek adorned with the beginning edge of a beard that had started to become salted. The features were undeniably masculine.

Auckland's put on some weight, she thought to herself, a hand on her forehead and stomach as she tried to force her mind to reconcile the images that so vastly betrayed what it was expecting. Whenever she used these devices, she always regretted whatever her last meal was. The waves of nausea that overtook her made it difficult to keep anything of substance down. As frequently as she had been using them in the past two weeks, her appetite had dwindled significantly. It didn't help that of the six sets in existence, her palantírs were the only ones that were implanted opposite of the rest.

A sharp sound broke her out of her thoughts. Displayed now was the form of a Xen'wa, even more brightly colored than Stresi, with several rings dyed around their wings. The Xen'wa's feathers were almost entirely given to oranges. It made a flicking

79

motion and a large image of a beautiful red planet appeared in the air behind. She was forced to watch as her perspective shifted, Auckland's focus moving onto a large box in front of where the Xen'wa spoke, causing Boer's stomach to reel once more. She recognized it as one of the Thlassian translation devices, though the older, more widely spread model. The world blurred once more as Auckland again shifted his focus back to the planet.

Taking in its red swirls, it took her a minute to recognize it. Gliese Prime, still drifting innocently out in the far reaches of space, the red star embracing it with its soft glow. The entire scene was quite beautiful, it peacefully drifting out in the stars, the system's star bathing it in its warm love. As the planet turned, one of the oceans was beginning to come into view, around it a small wreathing of green from the efforts to add life to the planet. A lone cloud drifted into view, testament to how far along the terraforming had come.

"This was captured by one of our ships in the area," came the Xen'wa representative's voice.

A moment later, a white streak pierced from the edge of the display, cutting right through the planet before vanishing on the other side. Boer watched, the image burning into her mind, as the planet seemed to get sucked into its center for a moment. A ring of debris erupted from behind the planet as another of dust and stone began circling around the point of impact. Boer listened as the chamber echoed with sounds of horror at the display. All she could do was watch two hundred and forty years of terraforming die. The planet began to crack, great scars separating the body of the massive planet until shards, each large enough to hold the hopes of future generations, jettisoned out into space. The Xen'wa representative motioned, and three more planets joined the display, each a beautiful jewel in its own right. Each pierced and killed by the same flash of white.

"What you have seen here is a weapon being used by the Terrans. By our estimates, the casualties on these worlds can only be calculated in the billions." The display changed, back to the remains of Gliese Prime, now resembling an expanse of asteroids, floating chaotically as they sought to return to some form of order.

"This was taken one stardate later." The Xen'wa paused, allowing the audience to process. "The Terrans have destroyed four worlds, two of which were habitable by most of the species present here. Two were near habitable. They have completely destabilized the gravitational balances of the systems in which they were housed. It is likely that more will be lost as a result of these systems becoming unstable. I call on the council to hear the Terrans answer for this travesty. "

Boer closed her eye, the image of the planets still etched in the darkness. In her ear, the voices of the council echoed on. When she heard Auckland's even keeled voice, distorted as it was through his perception, she focused back in.

"There was no crime here. Might I remind you all, when we joined the Council through payment of rip drive technology, we were afforded territorial concessions. These included the two systems that these planets resided in. When we took them over, we set upon terraforming them, at our own cost. We were given barren rock, devoid of even atmosphere. If they were habitable, it was because of our efforts. Second, there was no loss of life. The Terrarch made the decision thirty star dates ago that continued terraforming was infeasible. A full evacuation of the systems was rendered. These planets were empty of life. Third, our esteemed colleague suggests that these four planets were attacked by a weapon. Humanity possesses no such weapon. This was a mining device." Before he could continue, the Xen'Wa representative interrupted.

"A mining device!? What kind of fledglings do you take us for, Auckland!?" For his credit, Auckland did not lose his keel. He waited for a moment, letting the silence build, before flicking his hand. Where once was the projection of a shattered planet was now a heavily redacted blueprint for a space vessel. A quick look at the measurements placed it at monstrous proportions.

"What you see here is the *TSS Zaibatsu.* Inside Terran

space, we employ a recognized and approved mining technique, planet cracking. Most of you are aware of this technique, but have dismissed it as being too costly to implement. We have simply optimized the method of actually doing so. The *Zaibatsu* fields a fleet of thirteen hundred mining vessels, which will work on mining the minerals and valuable metals from the debris. It is one of four such vessels that we possess. We will begin mining operations in ten stellar dates. Might I remind the Xen'wa representative of the Galactic Terms of Engagement?"

The council fell silent, until a small voice spoke up from the far side of the chamber. As Auckland turned, a small construct came into view, not unlike the one that stood outside Boer's quarters.

"Might I inquire: Does the Xen'wa representative have evidence that the planets were, in fact, inhabited at the time of demolition?" The chamber turned, before the Xen'wa representative settled on his roost. "Very well, then. The Thlassian representative proposes that, potentially, there was no offense committed here. However, we strongly suggest that a formal investigation, led by a neutral third party, attempt to verify if these claims are true. As my species is currently brokering a treaty between these two parties, we shall abstain from leading said investigation." One by one, the other races slowly assented. They didn't want to risk angering the Terrans and severing their supply of drives.

The leader of this cycle of the council, the representative of Scretta, an insectoid-like creature that looked like a cross between a millipede and a gecko, spoke. "With that settled for now, let us depart, unless anyone else had something to bring before the council?"

"Sadly, I do," came Auckland's voice, and he stood, causing a retch to escape from where Boer lay. "As you are aware, tensions along the borders of Xen'wa and Terran spaces have been high as of late. Twenty one star dates ago, a Xen'wa warship rammed one of our orbital structures, deep in our territory. This sadly resulted in the loss of the lives of several of our people.

The Xen'wa have yet to answer for this. In addition, since then, a large number of their vessels have been systematically engaging and destroying defense vessels in the same region. The fact that the Xen'wa had these pictures to present to the council alone is evidence of this." Auckland paused, allowing the room to breathe. "We consider this an act of war."

The perspective shifted once again, bobbing and weaving as Auckland stood and began to walk. Boer couldn't resist the effect of the motions. This time, she couldn't help but let out a gurgle, the taste of vomit entering into the back of her mouth before she closed her eye. When she opened it again, Auckland was placing a large black leather binder onto the main podium.

"As such, we are issuing a formal declaration of war between our two species." Boer watched as the Xen'wa representative walked over to her. He stared directly into her eyes. When he raised one wing, for a moment she thought he meant to strike her. Instead, he jerked his head down, grasped one of his colorful flight feathers in his beak and ripped it out. He held it in his mouth and then spat it at her.

Slowly, she reached up one hand and ran it opposite over her skin once more, now slick with sweat. Her vision shifted back to the bulkhead over her bed. She opened her right eye, blinking it into focus before removing the plug. She barely made it to the bathroom before she lost her battle against her stomach.

Two rooms over, a construct worked its way around the diplomatic chamber. Painstakingly slow, it waved one of its appendages over the walls, a small light at its tip. It completed a full circuit of the room, before extending up towards the ceiling to continue its search. With both walls and ceiling clear, it repeated it once more across the floor, then the tank, then the perch, and finally the table. When it was scanning the underside of the table, it paused, before grabbing each of the legs with its lifter appendages, quickly turning the table in the air to look at its underside. On the gray metal table, nestled right by the corner closest to the tank, was a tiny black speck. The construct silently stretched one appendage towards the speck, before stopping. It remained like that for a while, motionless, pondering the implications of how it had eluded their notice, before withdrawing the appendage and carefully returning the table to where it was before descending through a near invisible door in the middle of the chamber.

After it had docked back into its charging station, the small Thlassian that had been controlling it floated down through the waters to join the commotion below.

Deep in the oceans of Thlassia, the two hundred gathered once more. They had been reviewing the data cachet that the Terrarch had sent. What they had seen unsettled them immeasurably. Due to its sheer size, they had divided up the responsibilities of analyzing humanity's history. What they saw was not a gentle thing. Each night, they had held a vote on a singular question, "Should we continue?" A singular thing threatened to push their answer one way. Another singular thing resisted it, and tried to push it the other way.

For every positive thing that they saw, dozens more examples were found of their barbarity. They were monstrous things, but also capable of great compassion. Throughout their discussions, they were joined by the twenty candidates that might one day join the two hundred, so that they may observe and learn. The importance of the task was too great to deny the future of their species the chance to have their opinions heard.

During the depths of the debate, one of their largest, oldest, and most venerable members had a proposition.

"There is a way that we might get a better measure of them," He had said, his deep call bringing silence with its echoes. He turned to the small form that had just arrived at the gathering. "It was proposed by my candidate."

CHAPTER TEN

"Only a fool loves their neighbor as thyself. We are a hateful, spiteful species. How many have died due to their own habits slowly killing them? How many have marched willingly to their own death for no greater purpose other than orders? How many castrate their own wills and desires on the altar of 'what's possible?' If we only loved our neighbors as though they were ourselves, we would have all killed each other a long time ago."
-- Wisdoms of the Terrarch

Mission report.

Slow. Progress is being made. I feel a resolution to my task may be upcoming.

Additional time?

Current projections should still suffice. If this changes, I will inform you.

We can only stall for so long. I have no desire to make this a protracted affair.

When Boer walked into the diplomatic chamber, she was alone. Getting back to sleep had been a difficult task, troubled as she was by her nightmares made real. When she began her ritual, sharply unclicking the briefcase and grabbing the first stack of papers, she paused, staring at the table. She stood like that, left hand full of papers while staring at the table for nearly a full minute. She reached out her right hand, placing it on the corner of the table, hand closed as though flipping a coin with her thumb extended. It groaned loudly as she gently pushed the corner forward slightly. Once satisfied, she began placing her documents out.

While she waited for her companions, she worked her way through the pages, reviewing her notes and thoughts on the various behaviors that she had seen sessions prior. When she reached the section on Gwooon's colorations, she paused. She felt strongly that she was missing something crucial in understanding Gwooon, some piece of him that would provide greater clarity to his actions. She thought on the visual display that Gwooon had had the day prior. Even more troubling was that for the first time, Gwooon had not come to speak with her during the night. She lost herself deep into thought, her eyes resting on the translator that was mounted to the edge of Gwooon's tank. She was still silently debating with herself when the back of Gwooon's tank opened up and he drifted in.

"Ambassador Boer," the device beeped to her. "As I am sure you are aware, it is unlikely for Ambassador Stresi to join us." She looked up at him. Startled, she took in the change to his form. On all days prior, he had been completely nude in the tank. Today, however, he had two bands of what appeared to be gold wrapped around each of his larger tentacles.

"We can both agree that it is understandable given present situations." She narrowed her eyes for a moment before deciding to press on. "Forgive me if this is forward. Might I inquire as to the bands? BOO-BOOP. Translator: Add Alternate -

Bands: A form of jewelry that takes on circular form, though is wider than a ring." Gwooon reached up a few of his smaller arms to gently tap against the metal bands, the tips of which flickered between orange and yellow. *Was that a motion of uncertainty?*

"This is the matter which I desired to discuss with you. I have received a request from deeper within my species. There is one which would converse with you, if you are agreeable to the notion."

Boer tilted her head in thought for a moment. *Perhaps progress is moving faster than I anticipated.*

"If I might inquire as to whom?"

"Consensus-elect Gwiiin. She is one that has been appraised as possessing the necessary qualities to join the Consensus in the future." Gwoon balled his tentacles up underneath his body. A ripple of color, a soft lilac, began at the tip of his tentacles and slowly waved its way across his body several times before he continued.

"She is my daughter." *Uncertainty? Pride?* "Since discussions are unlikely today, we wondered if you wouldn't be inclined to go on a .... walk?"

Boer's head reeled in surprise. "A walk?"

"Yes. We have constructed a walkway for you to enjoy. It is our understanding that your species does not tend towards confined spaces and thought that you might enjoy a ... change in scenery?" Boer chuckled internally, convinced further that she was indeed on the right path.

"It would be my pleasure, Gwoooon." She gathered her things up from the table and stowed them in the briefcase. "I assume the elevator will take me where I need to go when I am ready?"

"Of course, Ambassador Boer. At your leisure." Gwoooon turned to leave, then had a thought. "Boer?" She raised an eyebrow, a gesture that Gwoon had learned to recognize akin to the one the translator changed to 'May I inquire' when he was conversing with her.

"She is .... precious... to me." A flicker of yellow ripped

through him.

Boer held his gaze for a moment before bobbing her head, then turned to leave, thinking on why Gwooon would have felt the need to add that.

Once she departed from the room, Gwooon quickly worked his way through the watery tube that stretched out of the building, passing the guards that floated at its entrance before taking to the open water. The four guards trailed just behind him. Hurriedly, he jetted his way upwards, weaving through the water with anticipation as the colors in the water slowly blended back into the world as he approached the surface.

Stretching from the vertical shaft of the elevator was a new construction. As it stretched out into the water, it twisted and turned its way against the various structures of the dropoff before finally looping back to where the main shaft was anchored along the shelf. The entire thing was constructed out of a transparent material, allowing the natural golden light of their star to filter through. The bottom was slightly more opaque, but translucent enough for vision. Gwooon quickly approached the small cloister of bodies he saw. Upon arriving, he flicked greetings to the group before twining his two grappling tentacles with his daughter's for a moment.

"She will be arriving shortly," He motioned in the water, his smaller tentacles dancing with the movements. As his guards joined the ones around Gwiiin, they each dropped into formation, their colors shifting until they were almost invisible in the water.

The pair did not have to wait long before the door to the elevator opened and Ambassador Boer walked out. She had changed her attire. Before she had been clothed in plain garments that closely fit her form, neutral in coloration. She was now attired in a garment that billowed out from her lower portion. It swirled with oranges, whites, and blacks. It was long enough that the lowest portion of it teased sweeping against the floor. She had also fashioned her hair into a tight cluster at the back, two golden, metallic lengths piercing through it. Her briefcase was nowhere to be seen.

Boer looked for a seam where the walkway connected to the elevator shaft, but could only find the smooth curve of the wall. Not wishing to delay, she turned and took a few steps out. A small construct equipped with a translation device detached from the wall, falling in just slightly behind. For a moment, she paused, face turned upwards with eyes closed, her face highlighted by a flickering beam of light that came from the surface of the water. The pair waited for her to resume. Opening her eyes, Boer turned to Gwiiin and took her in. Like her father, Gwiiin also had the gold bands around her larger tentacles, though she had a further three small gold clips around her frill at the three, nine, and twelve positions. Her body had a blue flecking to it, unlike her father's gray-blue with green. What struck Boer the most was that Gwiiin was barely a third of the size of her father. Boer was unsure if this was an indication of age or a gender difference. She decided it didn't matter overly much, and respectfully curtsied towards her, opting towards formality.

"I thank you for this opportunity," she said, turning to begin the walk. When Gwooon had mentioned that they had constructed a walkway, Boer had been uncertain. She had a geological map provided to her, complete with a projection of the diplomatic offices. It was situated on the side of a great vertical drop off, the two long elevator shafts that came down from the landing pad reconnected at the bottom in the small complex that formed the diplomatic chambers. She had supposed that there wasn't much to see.

When she gazed through the transparent walls, she confirmed her earlier thoughts. The scenery around the tube was mostly that of the dropoff's edge, a barren rocky landscape that was only dotted with the occasional fronds slightly bent in the currents of the water. On the other side, the endless murk of open water. She noted that the Thlassians were on the side of the dropoff.

They walked in silence for a few minutes, approaching a

spot where the path veered sharply so that Boer could not see where it continued, blocked by a large boulder on the edge of the dropoff. Gwiiin was the first to break the quiet.

"I wanted to thank you for taking up our offer to host the talks," she said simply.

"The offer was certainly a surprise." Boer glanced towards them. "A pleasant one though."

The Thlassians were one of the smallest members of the Council, possessing a mere three worlds, only one of which was inhabited, Thlassia Prime, as the Terrans referred to it. They were also the newest species in the Council, having purchased their membership less than fifty cycles prior. All species seeking membership had to proffer some form of technology that would be of the benefit of the whole council. When the Terrans had joined 240 cycles ago, they had proffered the Rip Drive technology, enabling for the first time faster than light travel across the stars for the council. Prior to that, all travel had to be done at sublight, resulting in consequences with relativistic travel.

After the Rip Drives were introduced, this issue was alleviated. While not a panacea to the distances, chaining jumps allowed travel while minimizing relativism. Crews got their friends and families back. The Terran Federation had been voted in unanimously. The Thlassians were a much closer affair. Many deemed their proffer insufficient, though the deciding vote came down to the Terrans. Boer eyed the translation box over her shoulder.

"Do you have an interest in the translation devices?" Gwiiin asked.

"I do. Translation - Pitch up 10% last speaker," Boer replied, quickly adjusting how the device would translate Gwiiin's messages for her so that she would not sound identical to her father. "They truly are intriguing devices. It's most impressive how they can handle translating for all present, despite differences in biology."

"It was something that the Consensus focused on for quite

some time. One hundred and twenty seven of your earth years, if I am not mistaken with my calculations."

"This is the second time I've heard reference to this Consensus. I was wondering if I might inquire?"

"Certainly. The Consensus is something of great importance to our species. It comprises two hundred of our greatest members. Exemplar for all of our kind. They gather to provide guidance and leadership."

"You, yourself, are nominated for the Consensus, are you not?" One of Gwiiin's eyes rotated to look at her father before a lilac wave overtook both of their bodies. "It is a great honor, is it not?"

"While we do not have a direct parallel to that concept, I do believe that may be accurate." Gwiiin paused for a moment before adding, "I had exceptional teachers."

Boer paused her walk, and turned to face Gwiiin fully.

"We have a similar concept however." She let out a series of lower pitched noises. "It is a sense of fulfillment through being of service to others. It is considered one of the deepest callings of our people." They looked at each other for a few moments, the silence stretching, before Boer turned and resumed her walk.

This time, she was the one who found it important to break the silence.

"The Terrans found it disgraceful that more of the Council did not deem your proffer adequate." Out of the corner of her eye, she caught a slight twitch go through Gwiiin. "In our world, we have a field of study that we call 'Semiotics.' Are you familiar with it?" Boer waited, but nothing came. "I won't tire you with the details, but it consists of seeking to analyze the meaning behind all things, intended or not."

Gwiiin drifted alongside the tube for a moment. "A worthy pursuit. Does your species focus on this?"

Boer thought hard on this, her steps pausing. She was almost to where the tube bent.

"Probably not as much as we should." Boer sensed an

importance to the moment. Different paths flicked through her mind before she settled on her next words. "Many technologies have been proffered by species as they joined the council. Effective terraforming. New materials. Technological breakthroughs that led to the betterment of all involved." She paused, licking her lips, a sharp expression taking her face. "Your race proffered something that sought to help species accurately understand one another. A powerful message in itself, wouldn't you say?"

A streak of deep blue flashed down the center of Gwiiin's body. It was edged with that same lilac from before. Boer watched as Gwiiin quickly composed herself. Without waiting for her to finish, Boer turned and resumed her walk.

Turning the bend, she froze, stunned. Silently, she raised one hand, as though she were brushing away some moisture from her left eye. Her finger made a quick swipe on her brow as she moved her hand past. She knew who she needed to share this with.

Across the systems, five people suddenly reeled as their world shifted. Most of them, the message was not intended for, however, they would also receive it. It allowed a few of them to re-evaluate themselves. For the intended one, it was a message of great compassion, something that Boer understood immediately had been earned from a lifetime of service.

Before them was now a dazzling field of color and vibrancy. Great towers of red and blue, with tiny piscatorial shapes darting in and out of their small holes as they shimmered in the light. Great fronds waved in the ebb and flow of the water, dancing darkness across great swatches of smaller, more delicate whites, golds and bronzes that twisted and turned along the shelf floor. Large bowls that had entire schools cradled delicately inside their neon green edges. Creatures of all manner of shade and shape drifted through the waters, adding to the vibrant tableau before her. Boer could see the forms of dozens of Thlassians darting in and out, gently brushing the fragile structures, tending to them with the most delicate of touches.

In front of her, the life of Thlassia's oceans played and danced, cavorted and darted. Boer took that drop of compassion and joy that the Thlassians had intended for her and passed it on to the one who needed it.

Naked in her medical bed, the Terrarch closed one eye. Her aged and skeletal form had dozens of small metallic ports with thin tubes connected, each filled with the various medicines and chemicals that kept her exhausted organs barely functional.

Her mind jumped back centuries ago as the images from Boer flooded her. It brought her back to the time when she was a small child, floating along the surface, staring down at a similar world. As her mind processed the memories, the image of the child had changed. It was no longer her looking down at the world below, but a small child wrapped in a blue hospital gown.

As a thin line of moisture made its way through the valleys and crevices of her face, she heard a voice cry out over the soft beeping of the monitors.

"I'm fine. Continue with the procedure."

Slowly, with the images of that watery tapestry before her, she succumbed to the darkness of the anesthesia.

"Are you distressed?" came Gwiiin's voice, jolting Boer from her reverie. She raised her hand to her left eye again, quickly and subtly tapping the command to sever the connection. "Has the nursery distressed you? We can block it from view if you wish."

"No!"

Boer's voice had come out a little too forcefully.

"No ... No. It is fine," she said, composing herself. She placed a hand on her stomach and took in a deep breath. A soft smile overtook her face and she looked back out at the nursery. "I was simply … unprepared."

"I apologize. It was not my intent," Gwiiin intoned quietly. They both drifted quietly for a while, each in their own way. Boer stared back out at the life that was laid out before her.

"We called it Coral," Boer finally said, her voice low. Gwiiin turned to her. Gwiiin wanted to inquire further, but she felt she needed to allow the moment to mature. "I had never seen it before for myself. It was simply something that the Terrarch had shared with me a long time ago. Though the Terrarch tried her best, her words didn't quite do it the justice it deserved. I wasn't prepared to encounter it. Our planet lost it so long ago."

Boer looked out across the field of life before her, her eyes passing over and following the small forms that worked their way in and out of the crevices.

"Our actions at the time were …. foolish and hasty. We were … *poor hosts*." It was a calculation, trying to imitate the same sounds that Gwooon had used days prior. She hoped her readings into the implications of the translator's intonation were correct. Gwiiin watched her carefully, digesting Boer's use of one of her own words.

"It is one of humanity's greatest sins."

As the walk came to an end, Boer stepped into the elevator without a word. They had spent the rest of the walk in silence, Boer weighed down by the past, Gwiiin the deep blue of thought. The construct silently attached itself to the wall and the door hissed closed.

Gwooon's voice rang out while his skin danced in the deepest of purples. "Well done," he said simply, embracing his daughter once more.

I am requesting full authority to see this through.

Granted.

Boer?

Thank you.

CHAPTER ELEVEN

"The most important thing in life? To listen.
When you grab the hot pan, listen when it tells you its heat.
When the knife bites into your hand, listen when it tells you its edge.
When the darkness seeks to envelop you, listen when it tells you it is
dangerous.
Listen.
...and learn"
    -- Wisdoms of the Terrarch

S ure enough, ten star dates after the council met, the capital ship of the Xen'Wa fleet detected the gravitational anomaly of an incoming rip jump. They had taken up position in the debris field of Gliese, tucking their ships up against some of the larger chunks as they continued to drift. Pleased with his course of action, Commander Sasa preened. He had at his disposal a full third of the fleet, ready for the ambush. The Terrans would have no indication of their position, masked as they were against the rocks. They would be blind to sensors should a scan seek to reveal them, shielded by the corpse that the Terrans had created.

He watched through the display as space warped and distorted before an explosion of gravitational radiation announced the arrival of the *TSS Zaibatsu*. As the sensors took in the sheer size of the ship, Sasa let out a chirp, stretching it out before speaking.

"It's not often that you see something like that, fledglings." He turned to his sensor command officer. "Everything as expected?"

"Dimensions are matching that of the *TSS Zaibatsu.* I am registering no atomic signatures of any kind. They appear to be orienting themselves to approach the debris field."

Commander Sasa eyed his prey carefully, fluttering gently with anticipation. He had positioned his ships correctly. In moments, the trap would be sprung and his fleet would descend upon their prey, capturing a large portion of the Terrans' mining capabilities. It would be crucial towards forcing their capitulation.

"They will be in range shortly."

Sasa turned to his vice-commanders, and they quickly moved off to assume command of each of their squadrons. The ships present consisted of thirty five frigates, each with an accompaniment of ten destroyers and one hundred fighters. The unarmed mining ship stood little chance, despite its size.

Moments before it passed the engagement point, the sensor officer spoke out once more. "Sir, gravimetric distortion is off, the ship is carrying more mass than expected."

"Factor?"

"32% elevated."

"It's likely carrying minerals from its last endeavor. Task the boarding party with securing them when the time comes." The ship slowly drifted past the engagement point. Commander Sasa, resigning himself to the violence ahead, gave the order.

As one, the fleet took flight, leaping from their nests in the debris as their engines spooled up, launching them towards their prey. They were able to close half of the distance before sensors picked up the *TSS Zaibatsu* launching ships of its own. Five ships detached from its side, each slightly smaller than the Xen'wa's frigates. Sasa marveled at how blind the Terrans were, proceeding with launching their mining fleet. They openly declared war, in doing so making a vessel such as this a valid military target. Did they really think that the Xen'wa wouldn't retaliate and deny them the remains of the planet?

Most importantly, did they not have sensors to show that the attack had been launched? Only the greatest of fools would make a blunder such as this!

"Destroy all but one of those smaller ships as you approach the main. Capture the last," he ordered, already starting to think of the aftermath.

"Sir, another anomaly on those smaller ships!"

A display popped up, a magnified look at one of the smaller vessels. It was largely rectangular shaped, the edges smoothed with soft curves. The light of its engines could be seen radiating at the back of its small end. Down its side he could see the terran script spelling out *TSS Stiletto* down its side, though he had no idea what it actually meant. All over its hull, tiny spherical bumps textured the vessel.

Sasa narrowed his eyes, wondering at their purpose when, in mass, they detached from the ship before vanishing with a quick burst of light from engines contained within the spheres. Those spheres moved impossibly fast. No organic could survive that acceleration.

The screen quickly zoomed out so that Sasa could see the entirety of the situation. He watched in horror as the objects darted in between his ships. Great rips appeared in their structures shortly thereafter. Invariably, the spheres were crippling his ships before moving on to their next prey. This was a trap, but Sasa was wrong in assuming that it was of Xen'wa make.

"Sir, they are using kinetics!"

"Begin evasive maneuvers!"

He watched as dozens of his ships went adrift, their back portions torn asunder as the terran's kinetics ripped through engine bays.

"Ineffective. Casualties: 15% and rising." Sasa paused, frozen by the turn of events. "18%!"

Snapping out of it, he settled at what he must do. He had

hoped to take the vessel as a prize, but its complete destruction would have to suffice.

"Order retreat. All standby vessels are to commence atomic bombardment, full volley."

As one, the remaining ships of the fleet, all 35 frigates, detached from their perches. Their missiles joined the volley as hundreds of atomics launched from the bays of the vessels before orienting themselves towards their prey.

Instantly, both fleets began to disengage from each other. The Xen'wa ships that were still capable fanned out off the plane of the battle, clearing the way of the volley. The Terran ships recalled their strange orbs, before turning and beginning a full burn back to the *Zaibatsu*.

One ship, however, was slow in retrieving its spheres. Sasa observed the moment that they came to this realization, their ship flipping and burning away off plane from the *Zaibatsu* instead.

When he shifted the focus to view the *Zaibatsu*, he stilled. Blazoned across the hull of the ship were the terran symbols that *did not* spell out *TSS Zaibatsu* as he had anticipated.

He watched as the four smaller ships burned towards it, on an apparent collision course. Before they collided, small openings appeared in the hull of the mighty vessel, each ship flying inside before sealing up once more.

As one, hundreds, if not thousands, of smaller ports opened up as kinetic batteries appeared all along its hull. They immediately began launching their salvos, large masses hurled outwards into the void.

Many of them found their targets as the atomics were smashed to pieces. Even so, the onslaught of the missiles was too great. The entirety of the vessel disappeared behind a wall of light so bright that Sasa had to look away, his eyes struggling to focus due to the sheer brilliance of the glow. When Sasa turned back, he took in the result of his bombardment.

Across the once smooth hull of the ship were dozens of craters blown into the armor. The once uniform ship was now littered with a pox of shiny metallic spots, each where an atomic had successfully connected with the ship.

But it was still there.

Before Sasa could inquire as to confirmed breaches, the sensor officer spoke once more.

"Gravimetric anomaly consistent with rip jump!"

Sasa turned back to the screen and watched as the *TSS Destiny's Spear* disappeared just as it had arrived.

It hadn't taken the Xen'Wa long to remember the *Stiletto*. When they located it on their sensors, they saw it adrift.

Their engines were rent, the apparent result of one of their spheres attempting to return colliding with it. Around it was a field of spheres, all inert, the shattered one still drifting just behind the ship's ruined engines. They had cautiously flown towards them, wary that they might rearm, but the vessel seemed disabled as it spiraled in its off-axis spin. There were no transmissions from it of any kind, though it was clearly leaking a large amount of fuel.

Docking with it took some effort.

Stabilization of the prize took Sasa's crew longer than he cared to admit. With the spin finally neutralized, a smaller shuttle was sent out to attach to the hull and cut its way in. This, too, had taken far longer than expected. When they collected the crew, they departed and made their way back.

Sasa was apoplectic about the report.

Ten crew.

After carefully combing through the entirety of the ship, being careful to document every part of it, they had only discovered ten crew. An examination of their sleeping berths seemed to confirm this number. Sasa couldn't grasp how a ship of that size, with that capability, only required a crew of ten.

Discovered might not have been the correct word. When

his crew dropped into the ship, all ten had been lying prone on the ground, motionless with their fleshy, clawless limbs clasped behind their head. He ordered them brought to the bridge immediately as he relayed his findings to his superiors. What they would make of it, he had no idea. Per orders, he left a feed going from his bridge as they were led in.

Their hands were bound in front of them, still wrapped by the lightweight cuffs that the shuttle carried. They had been fully searched, anything that could be construed as a weapon confiscated and set to be examined at a later date. The only thing that was left for them was their uniforms. All around them, the crew of his ship had donned their battlegarb, a thick breastplate made of their most durable metals to protect vitals. Even with this display of combat readiness, the Terrans walked in with their heads held high, defiant. One of them turned his head towards one of the monitors on the bridge.

"It was smart of you to surrender as you did," Sasa said proudly.

Upon speaking, the translator box he had set up began to work. The first of the Terrans turned toward him, breaking his gaze from the screen that displayed a starmap of the region. Great swatches of it were dyed in the colors of the Xen'wa and Terrans, with a tiny dot nestled within denoting the Thlassian territory. He had turned his head towards it the moment that he had stepped into the room and saw that it was displayed.

"You will be treated in accordance to galactic treaty. Your biological needs will be met and you will be given quarters in which to reside. Separately. Do you have any medical concerns that need to be addressed?"

The lead one, surprisingly the smallest of the ten, spoke, the edges of his lips curved upwards.

"I assume you have a live feed going to your superiors?"

Sasa couldn't form a response, taken aback.

"Good."

All expression drained from his face.

"The Terrarch sends a message: 'Complete Surrender.'"

As one, the Terrans pulled a portion of their uniforms off and dropped them to the deck. Sasa could only watch in horror as his men, too slow to react, struggled to bring their weapons to bear, the small devices beginning to unfold in midair. The devices dropped quickly, far too fast for the gravity well of the ship, before clanging metallically to the deck. A sharp whine, and suddenly all of the Xen'Wa of the bridge were wrenched violently to the deck by some unseen force, hollow bones snapping as they collided with the floor.

Their breastplates clunked loudly, deafeningly so. The entirety of the bridge crew now lay motionless on the floor as it was plunged into darkness, small electrical explosions occurring all around them providing the only light.

Outside of the ship, the Xen'wa fleet registered a simultaneous drop in communications with the flagship as it lost core power. Before they could react, their sensors screamed of an incoming rip jump. They didn't have time to avoid it as a large ship with three long protrusions appeared in the midst of their fleet. The gravitational wave of its arrival caused the ships of the fleet to suddenly lurch into their hollows, their hulls bending and contorting violently as they scraped against the rock, leaving them adrift.

Before the fleet could muster a response, the three long protrusions of the ship slammed down into the hull of their capital ship, violently tearing into it. It had latched itself onto the ship, cradling it in its embrace. Then, they both vanished, another shockwave further ripping through the fleet, finishing the Terran's prey.

Aboard the inert ship, Sasa could hear the heavy footfalls of the terrans as they moved about the bridge. He struggled through the pain of his shattered limbs as he tried to reach his sidearm. He wasn't sure how much of the darkness was the lighting and his own body shutting down. When he finally worked his talons around it, he couldn't move it. He tried to lift it, but it refused to cooperate. Much like his breastplate, it refused to budge from the metal floor. The world around him was swimming. He felt like he was tumbling through the air, all sense of direction gone. He slipped into unconsciousness.

An unknown amount of time later, Sasa returned to consciousness. Above him was a black haired Terran, leaning over his bound form. Sasa tried to struggle against the restraints, but they wouldn't budge and caused pain to shoot down his side. He felt strange, almost as though he were floating on a thermal back home. Everything had a soft, fuzzy edge to it.

He let out a loud squawk of pain as he desperately searched for something. He looked around the room.

What he saw horrified him.

He was in some kind of torture ward and the Terrans were slicing open his men. He watched as one of them was slicing into one of the wings of an officer, revealing shattered bone beneath, the feathers plucked and discarded. He looked back up at the Terran whose hair was the Xen'wa color for death.

"Welcome aboard the *TSS Mercy*," he said, his teeth bare and threatening to tear into him.

Sasa slipped back into unconsciousness.

Operation Kamikaze was a complete success. Their fleet is too heavily damaged to press on for the moment. They have retreated back to their core system for repair. Those without rip drives were left abandoned on the field.

I expect you to follow through,

Auckland.

By your will, Terrarch.

CHAPTER TWELVE

"Regrets? I have no time to indulge such things.
*Of course, I have them. However, should I spend time dwelling
on them, how will I ever have the time to ensure they never happen
again?"*

    -- Wisdoms of the Terrarch

Ambassador Stresi was the first to arrive. Boer was not surprised by this, however, she was saddened by how long it took for this meeting to be called. It had been a full three star dates since Operation Kamikaze. The Xen'wa's capital ship, which the Terrarch had taken to referring to as The Magpie, since its name wasn't pronounceable by the human tongue, was now nestled neatly in a berth in a Terran shipyard. Already, engineers were working across it.

When she opened her door, she saw that Ambassador Gwooon was likewise arriving. He had removed the golden bands he wore last they met. On Stresi's side, he was once more wreathed by his guard. The colors of his plumage had changed. Before they were a dazzling display of red and oranges. Now, they were varying shades of black and gray, starting lighter up towards his neck and darkening as they progressed further and further down his body. The plumage on his head, usually standing erect, was now pressed flat along the nape of his neck. It had a sheen to it. Boer assumed it was something akin to hair gel.

"Ambassador Gwooon, Ambassador Stresi," Boer said curtly as she took her seat. She opted to take a move from the Thlassian's playbook and fell to silence.

They sat like that for a while. Boer calmly looking over at Stresi. Stresi looking back, as though trying to will his eyes to conjure the means to burn their way through to the back of Boer's skull and leave her twisting in the throes of death. When Stresi could take the silence no longer, at last he spoke.

"Your people will return it and prostrate themselves before us. They shall grovel for the mercy of the Queen." Stresi began hopping back and forth one leg, as if barely restraining himself from taking flight. Boer elected not to respond.

"You will do so, or we will bring the full wrath of our fleet down upon your homeworld. We will leave it barren, a wasteland not even fit for the smallest of grubs to squirm in. We will tear your precious Terrarch's flesh from her bones an…"

Boer's expression hardened and she opened her mouth to respond, before the translator suddenly cut Stresi's words off, leaving him chirping and tweeting at her. Boer looked at him for a moment, taken aback by how comical the display now was.

The Xen'wa in the chamber suddenly pulled themselves back, reeling as though under some pain. Boer glanced over to Gwooon's tank and saw that he had one of his tentacles extended, pressing on one of the joints where his berth connected to the wall.

"I will remind you a second time, when both parties agreed to us hosting the negotiations, a certain degree of civility and propriety was expected. I do not wish to have to remind you of this again." Gwooon's tentacle retracted back to his body, red sparks twisting their way across his skin.

Stresi leveled his gaze to where Gwooon gently floated, the red slowly calming away. Boer could sense him seething with emotion on his roost. Without another word, Stresi hopped from his perch and made towards the door. Before he could step through it, Boer finally spoke.

"Stresi." The Xen'wa turned. "I would remind you of the Terrarch's message."

Stresi remained in the doorway for a moment or two. Without a word, he turned and walked through.

"No, that is called a 'Bishop'," Boer said, her voice edged with humor. Before her, a metallic chess set, each of its pieces arrayed neatly into their rows. She reached forward to the metal chessboard, her hand brushing aside the metallic manipulator that was pointing to the piece before picking it up to move it to the center of the board.

"It's not the most powerful piece, per say, but it is dangerous nonetheless. When it moves, it does so."

She moved the piece on each of the diagonals.

"However, if used correctly, it can be vital to securing important territories of the board." She grabbed a rook. "Both of these pieces serve well in that role, protection, though you can also use them to attack."

"And this?" came Gwiiin's voice, moving the tentacle to be overtop another piece.

The day after their walk, a construct had arrived at her quarters. Boer had expected it to be manned by Gwooon, but was pleasantly surprised to find that it was Gwiiin. Gwooon had yet to return to her quarters. Instead, his daughter had taken over the responsibility of their conversations. Boer found herself actually quite pleased with the sudden development. With it, the nature of the conversations had fundamentally changed.

Boer felt fondly towards the past three star dates. They had spent much of the time conversing, swapping tidbits of their species back and forth. Boer welcomed the distraction, the strange new courses that their conversations would take. With Gwooon, the conversations had been meaningful, but were largely the type that occurs between academics, discussing thoughts and insights on advanced topics. They were extremely focused and limited to the topic that had been chosen. The conversations with Gwiiin were vastly different, more akin to an equal student, to keep the line of thought going. It was a much more relaxing, enjoyable affair. They would twist and wind, incorporating dozens of topics before eventually losing their way and just become an enjoyable exchange between two people. Even now, the topic had shifted to common games that were played among the species. Boer had described Chess to her, and a construct had come in with a board that closely resembled what she had described.

"That is a queen. It can move on any straight line, be it forward, backward, or a diagonal, from its position."

"Queen? Might I inquire: This is the title of a female ruler, is it not?" Gwiiin replied, a shadow of blue crossing over her form.

"It is, but a hereditary one." Boer paused, rethinking her words. "Historically, however, it was the title of the female spouse of the hereditary ruler, though there are notable examples of queens who held their thrones of their own right."

"Might I inquire: This is not unlike your Terrarch, is it not?" Boer froze, her thumb playing against the cool metal of the bishop.

"There is a core difference. A queen is generally not chosen. While some eventually came to be loved by her people, the fact is that they were not selected by those that served under her.

"The Terrarch rules because she has the full respect and support of all of humanity. We choose to follow her. We trust her guidance. We value her insight. We choose the path that she charts. With each passing moment, we reaffirm that choice."

"Might I inquire: How could she have possibly garnered such love?"

Boer paused, twisting her head to look out into the darkness of the waters beyond. Ever since they had shared their walk, she had left the curtain for the window open. Even now, she caught the glimpses of shapes flitting about the darkness, attracted to the light. They were no longer distressing to her.

"She united us," she finally said, her voice quiet. Gwiiin picked up that there was more meaning to the word that she had used than what the translator was providing her. There was a weight to it, as though the word had held both light and darkness. Gwiiin allowed Boer to pause a moment longer while she waited for her to elaborate.

"You must understand. Our history is not a pretty one. We were not always a peaceful species. At times, war, conflict, and violence come as easy to us as breathing. She came to us at a time when we had, once again, pushed our world to the ultimate precipice."

Boer stared at her reflection in the glass, a shadowy figure that loomed over the dark shapes in the water. "Did you know that out of all of the species on the council, humanity was the only to develop atomics prior to spaceflight, let alone colonization of another celestial body? Not only that, when we had invented them, we didn't stop there. Our violence was not yet satiated. We pushed it further, eventually finding subdivisions within them, fission and fusion, weapons so great that they could extinguish the life of millions in a single burst."

Her mouth went dry before she continued. She glanced over at Gwiiin, who was motionless on the screen, her form nearly invisible as she perfectly matched the water that was around her. Boer couldn't stand looking at Gwiiin hiding herself, so she turned back to the darkness.

"The greatest threat humanity has ever faced has always been humanity itself. We have a viciousness that runs through us. Likely due to environmental pressures on our evolution, but it is a part of us nonetheless. It shapes us, forms us, envelops us as completely as your waters do you.

"For most of our history, we endeavored to keep ourselves in separate, well-defined groups. We defined these lines with whatever terms were deemed appropriate for the age. Race, gender, religion, sexual orientation, class, intelligence, wealth.

Anything that we could use to define something as 'other', we did. Atomics were already being used against groups that fell into that classification of 'other.' The amount of loss was ...

"It was a dark time.

"It was then that she came to us through the darkness: a beacon of what we could be. She reminded us of something that we had long forgotten. We could be more. We could do more, see more, accomplish more. We didn't have to focus on the divisions that separated us. She taught us to look past them, beyond them for something more. She was a thing of fierce will and determination that cowed that violence in a way that had never happened before. She reduced us to our very core and showed it to us.

"You know, we once had an entire city, filled with people like her. People who could be offered everything that they could have ever dreamed of, but would just reply that it would be better to die *for* than to rule *over*. People who lived by their convictions instead of simply voicing them. People who had built their entire society around those convictions.

"But the city came far too early in our history. Time erased it. She reminded us of them, of their conviction. She took it upon herself to unite us, to forge us back to what they once were. She made it so that we could never forget them again. Her own convictions became our guide.

"One by one, those divisions that had once seemed impenetrable began to fall. Some by force. I won't deny it. It is the core of who we are. Most, however, fell through choice. They chose to set aside their weapons and instead look for something they recognized in each other.

"For the only time in our species history, we stood as one, united. Whole and complete... Terran."

The conversation lapsed into silence after that, neither side willing to violate it. They sat like that, swimming in their thoughts as time passed by.

Eventually, Boer heard a soft metallic click behind her. Turning, she saw that the board had changed. Gwiiin had moved the black pawn from e5 to e7. Boer smiled.

"Black should always go last," she said, before meeting her with her own.

Hours later, after Gwiiin's construct had already left, Boer was busy cleaning up the pieces and stowing them away in her luggage when she heard a tapping noise on the glass of her window. Turning, she saw Gwiiin's form illuminated against the glass, the blue flecks on her frill glowing in the darkness. The construct, long since powered down in the corner of the room, came back to life. "I meant to inquire. What was the name of the city?"

A soft dampness came to Boer's eye.

"Sparta."

The two stared at each other for a moment through the small barrier before the construct powered down once more.

Boer turned back to the board and quickly stowed it, replacing it with her terminal. When she opened it and entered her credentials, her gaze landed firmly on the new icon she had noticed before Gwiiin had arrived earlier that day. It was a simple thing, nestled at the end of the different commands and functions that she had access to across the greater Terran network. Boer recalled the file that Fletcher had carried with him while she was still finalizing the plan. It had been so thin, yet had such a great weight to it.

The icon, simply a small square with one point upwards, a cross hanging from the point below, held a similar weight. The entire thing was red in color, representative of the blood that it could unleash. When Boer had requested full authority, she hadn't completely understood the weight of it. Now, as she gazed at the icon for ATHENA, she was beginning to understand the Terrarch's burden.

It threatened to swallow her.

Auckland?

Boer?

Notify them.

Are you sure?

By your will, Boer.

CHAPTER THIRTEEN

"Confliction and conviction. So similarly powerful, yet so profoundly different. One will swallow you, the other, crush you. It is up to you to decide which is which."
-- Wisdoms of the Terrarch

The Xen'wa representative paced in his office a few circuits, before taking a giant leap, wings flapping and landing on the high roost in the corner. If he was going to take this meeting, then he was going to be sure that he had the height advantage.

In walked, no, *crawled*, the Scretta representative. A shiver went down the Xen'wa's spine. He never could understand how a creature could get around solely by crawling, much less a sentient one. It was so... unclean.

The Scretta representative scuttled in, his main body writhing in a grotesque display with his movement, side to side. He was clad only in the hard exterior that he had as skin, resembling the color of a burnished stone, all mottled and hideous. Along his side was a procession of dozens of small leg stubs that ended in three large hooks, each of which could move independently. Part of the reason why the Xen'wa representative found the Scretta so abhorrent is that it had evolved to dominate a similar niche in ecology, but they had evolved along such a different path. Almost as a reflex, the Xen'wa representative puffed his chest and feathers out as the Scretta representative pulled his upper torso off of the floor so that he could turn his face upwards.

Both of them evolved to fill the tops of their trees. The xen'wa took on the full avian form, slowly developing the hallmarks of intelligence of millenia of evolution, the ability to manipulate objects, observe, joints that facilitated picking things up and examining them.

The Scretta, however, had evolved down the insectoid line. In their early days, their species would lurk in the canopies of their world, waiting for a creature to pass beneath before dropping on them and incapacitating them immediately. When their species had started to diminish the populations of prey animals on their world, the pressure had developed into sentience, allowing the species to eventually continue the hunt out in the stars, culminating in the technology of effective terraforming, the ability to develop planets to harbor life.

That development never ended. The Scretta had simply invented it out of necessity. Out of all the species, they spent the most on terraforming projects, constantly seeding new planets to build havens, filling them with dozens of species from the hundreds of worlds across the galaxy. They had one task for the worlds, make them perfect for the hunt. They lived to hunt, they yearned for it, they *were* the hunt.

Their drive to hunt was something that shaped their very society. Periodically, their species would, in sync, go into something they called the "Great Killing.' During this time, the only thing that would matter for the Scretta is the desire for prey. Everything would be the hunt, even allies. It was a time of great violence for their species, when the Scretta completely isolated themselves from as much as possible. They made the active choice to try and limit the casualties as much as they could. The only exception was their Hunting worlds. Entire worlds where every flora and fauna imaginable were dropped off and carefully balanced together, all so that the higher ranking Scretta could satisfy their urges in what were deemed a more 'natural' manner. Those worlds became drenched in blood and the screams of dying animals.

As it was, the Scretta representative was still in his docile state. The spines on the back of his carapace were still blunted small. When they lengthened, he would recuse himself from discussions and debates on the council floor, most of which would only be of local consequence and didn't involve the Scretta, until his hunting season was over.

The Xen'wa representative greeted his counterpart, opening his wings and dipping his head down low.

"Let us be quick about it," the Scretta representative clacked, the translator in the room having no problem interpreting the discordant noises into the Xen'wa's chirps and trills. "I have two matters which require stating. First, this issue with the Terrans. Resolve it. Quickly. We do not wish to see it escalate. Secure a treaty with the Terrans."

The Xen'wa representative switched which foot he stood on before responding.

"That is our intention. Talks have been ordered to continue on Thlassia."

"Good. Second, my servant will be sending over the list of systems that we will be hunting in this season. Two of them border your systems. With tensions being what they are, we felt it important that you understood."

There was little discussion after this. The Scretta were not a loquacious species.

An sat at the terminal.

He wasn't sure if she would answer him, after all that had happened. There was a time when she would have. There was a time when any issues that An had raised would have been heeded. When his insights carried so much weight that he could push anything aside and bring them to the forefront.

But that was before.

Now, as An sat at the terminal, looking over the plans, he realized how badly his 'indiscretion' had cost him. He had severed himself from the center of power. He suspected that any day now, the Terrarch would come to have his palantírs removed. He had decided that what would be, would be. He dedicated himself back to his work, starting with the plan. As he began to work his way through it, he was surprised by how measured it had become. He had been fearful that Boer would have made it so thoroughly entrenched with blood that just looking upon it would stain him. Now, however, he could see that she took almost every opportunity to avoid it. The ships were to target engines. They would use words to persuade instead of violence to force. It was a masterful attempt at peace. It used the violence it contained as an affirmation of the path that humanity had chosen into the stars. There was one problem, however.

He had noticed the issue late the day prior. Since then, he had been struggling with how to compose the message. Eventually, he decided he just needed to inform the Terrarch. If she took the communication stream, then he would tell her. If she didn't, he would try the others, consequences be damned. The Terrarch had made it clear that he wasn't to undermine Boer, but there was potential here. Dangerous potential. He needed to make sure they knew.

He tapped the keys to open the communication application. To his surprise, the Terrarch connected.

Terrarch?

She didn't reply. An waited at the terminal for more than two hours, but she didn't reply. She didn't sever the connection, either. He tried again.

Terrarch?

Again, he waited, to no avail. She was sending him a message with her silence. What that message was, he wasn't sure. He had no choice however, he would have to reach out to Boer if she didn't send a response. There wouldn't be enough time before the announcement for anything else. He wasn't sure if anyone would answer. He tried a final time.

Terrarch, please respond. It's urgent.

Do you know why I did it?

I am confused, Terrarch.

I am aware.
Do you know why I did it? The Cell?

I went against Boer...

Boer is irrelevant.

An leaned back.

Just like that, she had unmoored him again. An had assumed that it was done to teach him a lesson. Do not go against Boer. Clearly, that wasn't the case. Then why? Why had she stripped away the entire life that he had built for himself? Why had everything that he had in his life been so brutally riven from him and had he been abandoned adrift? What message was that supposed to send him?

It is clear to me now that I did not.

You were conflicted, An,
weak. There is no room for such
weakness at the moment.

I am old, An. I have seen
where confliction leads. You
had lost your understanding of
yourself. Down that path lies a
hard lesson.

May you never learn it.

He severed the connection. It was true. All of it. An thought of the spiral that he had been descending. He was about to act purely in fear when she intervened. She had saved him, in a way. He sat there, motionless, long enough for the screen to flicker to black as the terminal shut itself off due to lack of use. He continued to gaze into the black screen, his reflection staring back at him.

He knew what he had to do.

He quickly booted the terminal back up, keyed in his credentials, and opened a communication stream. The recipient did not hesitate to accept it.

Boer?

Speak.

Be careful of the Scretta.
No matter what, the most
important thing is that they
MUST NOT view us as prey.

CHAPTER FOURTEEN

"Be Direct."
-- Wisdoms of the Terrarch

S pecies of the Galactic Council, I thank you for joining me today," Auckland said, flicking through his binder.

"I will keep this brief. Effective immediately, the Terran Federation is withdrawing from the Galactic Council, in totality."

The entire chamber froze.

"All Terran civilians have already been relocated to Terran space. All properties in other species' territories have been sold to local figures. All contracts are canceled. All trade is hereby ceased.

"It is our wish to maintain an embassy adjacent to Council Headquarters. For the meantime, any entity that feels they have incurred some form of financial harm through this process may submit a request for compensation there. The Terran Federation will maintain ownership of all territories it currently occupies." He looked up to the motionless figures of the other representatives.

"That concludes my statement."

For the first time in the forty years that Auckland had been in the Council Chamber, it was so quiet that he could hear his footfalls on the soft floor. He had made it all of the way to the exit when a voice cried out. All around the chamber, he could see the stunned forms of the representative species. Even the Scretta, a species that stayed in near constant motion swaying back and forth, was completely still. That worried Auckland. There was something on the very edge of his mind that An had once said that he couldn't quite grasp at.

"And should we not deem this acceptable? If the united fleet of the Galactic Council enters your home system and rains fire upon you, it does not matter how large or capable your fleet is! Your planets will be wiped from the charts!"

Auckland's ear buzzed. He paused but a moment before turning to the Scretta Representative.

"The Terrarch sends a message." He paused, a fierce flame taking over his eyes, the likes of which the council had never seen before.

"IF."

CHAPTER FIFTEEN

"Always doubt what you know.
Never doubt what you do not."
-- Wisdoms of the Terrarch

Sasa flinched as sent sharp pains raked their way down his side. When he recovered, he looked around at his men and reflected.

Since the complete capture of his vessel, he had been treated surprisingly well. According to council law, he was entitled to a few things.

The first was medical treatment for any wounds sustained during the capture. On this account, the Terrans had lived up to expectations. When capturing the ship, the victory had been absolute. Only a handful of Xen'wa had escaped without injury. An effort had been mounted immediately after the Terran's strange ship had ripped them out from amidst their fleet, but it was quickly dispelled with no loss of life. The Terrans had employed sonic devices to neutralize any efforts, pitched to not affect their own crew.

When the medics descended upon the crew, they were a deafened and motionless lot. Broken bones were the greatest concern for the Xen'wa, and the Terrans quickly set themselves to the task of taking them aboard another of their massive ships, the *TSS Mercy*, as it was called.

It bore strange symbols down its hull, fields of white with a splash of red that Fletcher had referred to as "a cross." They didn't stop at the injuries they were responsible for. Many of his crew were currently undergoing treatment for a litany of other concerns, be it genetic conditions, old injuries, or developing illnesses that members of his crew were not yet aware of. When the medical staff of his own ship had been patched up, the Terrans had integrated them into their own, allowing them the freedom to tend to their wounded brethren, an unheard of kindness amongst the fleets. There had even been interchange of various medical techniques between the two crews. Any requests for additional medical supplies were quickly rendered.

When it came time for the second obligation, quarters suitable to their species' needs, the Terrans had again exceeded expectations. It was the galactic norm to provide the minimum, generally tiny quarters in which to rest that provided the bare minimum needed to ensure the survival of the captive. Once again, the Terrans had not just exceeded expectations, but massively so.

Instead of cramped, isolated quarters, the Xen'wa had been led to a series of connected domes on the surface of their station. These domes were massive, each a great open space that the Terrans had adorned with foliage from their native world. Structures had been constructed across the expansive fields for the Xen'wa to reside in. The domes' tops were transparent, though a shield did occasionally work its way over, plunging the dome into a darkness that was close to dusk on his own world. Sasa had noted that the Terrans had synced these shields with a day-night cycle that would be comfortable to Xen'wa biology. Within the domes, his crew were given free-reign, permission to move about their dome, and even between domes. Understandably, that was the extent of their allowed ranges, as the Terrans had guards posted at the exits to the rest of the station. Even so, the unexpected freedom was welcomed. Despite the capture hanging like rain over his crew, morale was high as his men found themselves in conditions approaching leisure.

The quality of the rations only furthered this. On board the warship, rations ran towards the necessities, carefully manufactured in factories. Tasteless, dry things that provided an optimal replenishment to weight ratio. He watched as two of his men passed around something that the Terrans had called an "apple". Sasa's medics had been allowed to analyze any foodstuffs coming into the domes, ensuring that it was compatible with their people's biology. These apples were one of the foods that they accepted, though the medics had warned that they were slightly higher in natural sugars than the foods his crew were used to.

Naturally, they loved them. Each shipment had doubled in size, then doubled again as his men devoured these "apples."

Sasa turned to where Fletcher stood. Behind him stood one of his men, rolling around a cart that had one of the thlassian translation devices. Fletcher himself was dressed in a Terran military uniform, deep blues covered in tiny bits of metal that gleamed in the sunlight of the dome, adorned with strange markings that he had said indicated they were of a similar rank. Sasa thought back to when he had first seen Fletcher, still under the effects of the drugs that they had given him to help with the pain. He looked so remarkably different now.

"What did you want, Fletcher?" Despite the accommodations, Sasa couldn't find it in himself to be anything but terse with the man. The Terrans had utterly picked his plan apart. He had been so sure of himself, and the Terrans had callously outmaneuvered him as though he were a fledgling struggling with his wings for the first time. Everything since the formal start of this war had been fully controlled, manipulated, cultured by the Terrans. They had anticipated the trap, and laced it with one of their own.

Before the first volley had been exchanged, Sasa's defeat had already been so absolute and humiliating that he had considered denuding himself of his feathers in shame. It agitated him immeasurably.

"How are your men settling in?" Fletcher asked, ignoring the continued brooding of the Xen'wa commander. He was under no obligation to indulge Sasa's morose.

"The accommodations are far above expectations."

"Good," Fletcher turned to face. "Are you up for a bit of a walk? We could give you something for the pain, if it's a concern." Sasa waved him off, before the motion caused him to flinch from the pain that it sliced down his side.

"Suit yourself."

Fletcher didn't wait to see if Commander Sasa would follow. Instead, he turned and began leading him away. Sasa considered just watching him go. He had little choice, however, as two guards stepped up behind him. He received the message and fell in pace behind him.

In a way, Fletcher's actions since he had captured him and his crew surprised Sasa. He had assumed that Fletcher would immediately separate him from his crew for questioning, or something far more violent. It was standard practice amongst the various fleets to do so. It discouraged resistance. By forcing compliance, you addressed a litany of other issues that might arise. Maybe this was a ploy to separate him from his men now? Sasa didn't have an option though. He was completely at their mercy, his only real option was to follow.

They took a winding path, twisting and turning through the corridors of the station. Sasa was still unsure of the purpose of such a massive structure. He and his men were isolated to a small portion of it. What they could see through their domes was just empty space. The stars changed, but repeated, implying that they were locked in orbit around something. The station could have been anything. Habitation, detention, He simply didn't have enough information to understand why the Terrans would build something so massive out in space. He finally understood when they entered a hallway that was dominated by glass.

Through the window, he could see the massive form of his

warship, constructed in the form of a Xen'wa swooped to strike mid-air. All along its bow, he could see sparks flying through the air as Terrans worked on the ship, great cascades of light. His first impulse was that they were dismantling it. Anger welled up inside of him at the indignity, that they would chop apart the pride of the Xen'wa so flippantly. This was quickly replaced with confusion, as the Terrans lowered a massive metallic plate down to one of the rent portions of the ship.

As it was laid out flush along the damaged hull, sparks began flying as the Terrans set themselves to task. His mind couldn't understand it at first. Then it shot through him. *They were repairing it.* Why? Why would they be repairing their ship? The only answers that came to Sasa's mind were plans to use it as bait for a trap of some kind. He couldn't allow it.

"What is the meaning of this?" he cawwed down the hallway towards Fletcher.

Fletcher paused his step, then turned and faced him. Sasa's plumage had puffed out, his breathing elevated. Fletcher locked gazes with the avian. Sasa couldn't understand the expression on the man's face. If only he had some way of deciphering the Terran's intentions, however, they didn't seem to have quite as developed body cues as his own species did.

As they held their stare, Sasa felt his anger rise further, then slowly begin to float away. His plumage settled back down. There was no point in it, after all. If they decided to repair it, that was their decision. For all effects and purposes, that was no longer his ship. It was theirs. When his feathers had finally settled, Fletcher turned without a word and resumed his walk.

They worked their way through more and more of the shipyard. Sasa understood precisely the nature of this structure now, having seen his own ship berthed inside. It alarmed him how the chamber in which his ship was being worked on dwarfed it. It could easily have serviced two or three more. He also understood that he had no way of confirming if that was the only berth in the shipyard. Whatever the Xen'wa had thought about the Terran capabilities was sorely wrong and outdated.

They had assumed that all of their production was geared towards the rip drives. Structures like this, on this scale, only serve one purpose.

War.

As they walked, the hallways began to shift. What had started as a simple stroll through wide, open hallways laid with smooth and polished surfaces had given way to a far more industrial design. Often, much to the protestation of Sasa's body, they now had to duck and turn as they worked their way through pipes and past protrusions. They had entered into a functional portion of the shipyard. Gone were the comforts of design from earlier. Now, the only thing that mattered was purpose.

At last, they came to a sealed chamber, a metal ring set out from the door centered in the wall.

Fletcher stopped, stepping aside. Sasa stood there, staring at the door with apprehension. This door was not a thing of comfort. It was far too sturdy for that purpose. This left only one thing. They were indeed separating him from his men, hiding him away in the bowels of this massive construction.

To what purpose? Torture? Starvation? What punishment had they wrought for the enemy that had led their foe? He knew that he couldn't resist them. They had already won.

Defeated, he slowly approached the doorway. When he passed by Fletcher, a hand clapped down just before the joint where his wing connected with his torso, the sudden pressure sent a quick shock of pain down Sasa's side.

When Sasa turned his head, he was met with a gaze that pierced through to his very core. He understood in this moment that they had been wrong about the Terrans. The Xen'wa had been so sorely wrong. They had assumed that, due to their peaceful nature, the Terrans would not resist them. They had assumed that, when confronted with violence, they would yield.

They had assumed that violence was not their way.

Sasa understood now. The Terrans would not shy away from violence. They could not. They *were* violence. They embraced it fully. It was an integral part of them. At that moment, Ambassador Stresi's briefings echoed in his mind.

They were neither prey, nor predator.

No, they were something far, far more dangerous. They were both, yet simultaneously, neither. A predator that refused to be prey. Prey that had learned to embrace the violence of predation. A species that had to fight to survive at every turn. When they met a challenge, they had to meet it with utter brutality until their domination of their environment was so complete that all natural threats had been removed. Even then, they had held onto their violence. It had engrained itself into them too deeply. It was inseparable.

They had stepped into the stars in peace.

They were forged in violence.

Suddenly, Fletcher stepped back, brusquely removing his hand from Sasa's body so that he could stand stiffly, clasping his hands behind him.

One of the guards reached up and quickly spun the ring on the door. Sasa could hear heavy mechanisms at play behind it, and then the grunt as the guard swung the thick metal door outwards. Sasa closed his eyes, and stepped inside.

It was not what he expected.

Inside the room, there was only one source of light, a single dominating viewport set into the wall of the small square room. The corners of the room were pitch black in shadow. Sitting on a soft black couch was an elderly Terran, starkly pale in her white attire, extreme in her age. The skin of her mostly bald head was mottled with the effects of time, only a few thin wisps of white still desperately clung on. Two thin, twig-like arms were stretched before her, hands clasped atop a glass bauble mounted in a smooth black cylinder that stretched to the floor. Her skin hung loosely off her frame, as though time had emptied her out from within. She didn't turn to face him, her gaze fixed outwards through the window. Despite all of this, she radiated a power that cowed Sasa. He had only felt such a presence once in his life, years ago when he was granted his commission personally by the Xen'wa Queen.

Sasa recognized her immediately. Unbidden a thought entered into his mind. How easy would it be to charge forward and with a quick flash of his talons, tear open her throat. He would be hailed a hero back home. The Terrans wouldn't be able to stop him!

"You would be dead before you took a step," came the Terrarch's voice, still firm and hard despite the softening of time. She hadn't even bothered to turn her gaze. The shadows shifted in the corner of the room. He realized they were not alone.

She raised one arm, motioning to a small roost that was bolted to the floor beside the couch. It was far lower than a Xen'wa preferred, barely enough space between the bar and floor for him to put his talons, but he obliged anyway, pacing submissively over before settling upon it. They sat like that, in silence, staring out into the stars.

Arrayed before him, dozens of structures, similar to the one he now sat in, floated out in the emptiness. He could see each had four large cradles on the side, ships currently in construction. They were arrayed around the red planet below in a great ring, stretching out and past the horizon of the planet. Above and below was another ring, and another, and another. It was an unfathomable amount of production. This wasn't something that a species could build overnight. No, this was a generational effort. The ability to build fleets of astronomical proportions.

Yes. He understood them completely now. He was beginning to see the trap that they had laid.

His eyes eventually settled on a cluster of gantries that floated separate from the rest of the structures, on which the Terrarch's gaze was focused.

Unlike the others which he could see were currently set

to task on massive hulls, these sat empty. As they watched, a large portion of one of the gantries separated before a ship floated into view, two large flat extrusions pressing up against the now adrift piece. Both immediately disappeared from view, rip jumping away, leaving the rest of the structure untouched. In this massive field of production, only one thought could enter Sasa's mind.

These structures had already completed their purpose.

Sasa understood two things with this demonstration.

The first: there was no shockwave. The only way to detect a rip jump was through the sudden spike in gravimetric distortion, a byproduct of the violent way the drive spooled up a wave of gravity to tear through the fabric of reality. This wave rippled outwards, both at arrival and departure. It was this gravitational wave that sensors looked for to detect incoming or outgoing rips. The sudden gravity had the ability to rip and tear things near it asunder. The Terrans had the means to completely neutralize this.

They could be anywhere.

The second raked icy talons through his body, squeezing at the small heart that fluttered wildly in his breast. Clawing at his lungs. Freezing his vision. Tearing through his very existence. He felt his extremities going numb in a way that Sasa had never felt before, almost as though they were detaching themselves from his body as they tried desperately to flee from this great threat.

He sat, transfixed.

With effort, the Terrarch stood, removing herself from the black couch. She loomed over him.

"When the time comes, I want you to deliver two messages."

He stared out at the fifth and final gantry.

He listened.

While they guided him away, he followed meekly, thinking of the Terrarch's messages. At least they would be easy to remember. One was but a single word, the second a string of numbers that the Terrarch had elected to translate and place on "paper" for Sasa. He stowed it in his breastplate.

When he looked up, they had stopped in front of a door that he didn't recognize. This one did not have the heavy mechanism on it, instead it looked like one of the automated ones that the Terrans tended to favor. The door opened with a hiss. The inside was a stateroom only fit for a high ranking officer. Sasa looked at Fletcher, confused. He simply motioned him inside. Sasa looked at him for a moment, trying to judge his intentions, but then obliged.

When the door hissed shut behind him, he was surprised to find he was alone with Fletcher. Sasa understood though. What did a creature such as Fletcher, so thoroughly intertwined with violence, have to fear from someone wounded such as he? No, he was no threat to Fletcher. He might never truly have been.

Sasa looked around the room, taking it in. He quickly realized these were Fletcher's personal quarters. There were too many personal touches for it not to be. The uniforms hanging in the small closet, the photos that showed a younger Fletcher with some terran woman holding up two documents of some kind, a series of Terran medals along the wall. No, this was his room.

What caught his attention was at the center. A small table, checkered with black and white squares, one of the Thlassian translation devices set beneath it. On the board, thirty-two pieces of black and white, mirrored. Just as the pieces were on opposite sides of the board, so too were a terran chair and a Xen'wa roost. He looked at Fletcher in confusion. He simply shrugged.

"I'm pretty sure all the crew just let me win. There's really only one person that puts up a good fight of it, and she's been busy with everything that's going on," he said walking up to the board. He turned to him, a strange expression on his face. "I trust I won't have that problem with you?"

Sasa could only stare back, his beak hanging ajar. They stood like that for a long moment, before Sasa sulked over to the roost and settled down. Fletcher took a seat, opposite.

A few hours and an unfathomable amount of losses later, Sasa screamed, "I give up!"

He picked up a piece and slammed it down in the center of the board, causing most of the pieces to shake and fall. He regretted the action. It had once more sent flame dancing down his side and had revealed to Fletcher the degree to which he had so thoroughly been beaten.

Fletcher stayed calm at Sasa's sudden outburst, quietly reaching out and grabbing the pieces that had toppled over. He quickly returned all the pieces back into their starting positions, save the one that Sasa had slammed into the middle of the board.

"Let me go over the rules again." Sasa glared at him.

"This, here, is called a 'knight,'" Fletcher said, placing one of his soft fingers on the piece in the center of the board. He pulled his hand off the piece then placed it on his chin.

"Wait a minute, let me get something." Fletcher stood and walked to the desk at the side of the room. He lingered a bit, looking up at the picture of him and the Terran female. *Fondly?* Sasa asked himself.

Fletcher quickly went back to task, grabbing a large pad of some kind and a small metal cylinder. As he walked back, he put his thumb on the end and pressed down, a small click coming from it as something small and metallic poked out from the other end. When he sat back down, he brought the two together, the arm that held the cylinder moving wildly. When he finished, he turned the paper to face Sasa.

"See, Knight!" he said, running his finger under the strange terran script. Sasa looked at him in dumbfounded disbelief. Fletcher did it once more. "Knight!"

"Repeating it does nothing," Sasa said blandly. How had he

been beaten by this idiot? Writing its name in a script he didn't know.

"Oh, erm," Fletcher said, turning the pad back over and taking more motions.

Before he showed Sasa what he had written, he reached out and grasped the knight with one hand, sliding it to a black square. He looked up into Sasa's eyes.

"Just remember, it moves like this," he said, looking back down on the board. He slowly slid it towards Sasa two spaces, then one to the right, ending on a white square.

"You must always keep your eye on it. It attacks obliquely, in a way you least expect." He wiggled the piece in his fingers so that it danced within the white square. He removed his hand and held up the pad again. He had added only the most rudimentary of scratches to it. Only a fledgling would possibly call it a good representation of the knight. *Skies above, what wind could have possibly blown me here?* Sasa thought to himself.

Mercifully, he was saved when a sharp knock sounded on the door. A moment later, the door hissed open and a female terran officer stood in the doorway, saluting. Sasa recognized her, though she was older.

"Sorry, sir, I found a space in my schedule and we usually have our game around now." Fletcher returned the salute.

"It's fine. Guards! Escort Commander Sasa back to his men."

"Stop it!" Boer cried, tears struggling down her face as she writhed away from the construct. She desperately tried to smack it away, but it was to no avail. Despite her flailing arms, Gwiiin's control of the construct was far too adept, the metallic arms snaking and writhing betwixt Boer's, tips snaking forward to brush ever so softly down her side. As the next found its mark, it sent another involuntary spasm down her body, forcing more laughter from her mouth as she vainly tried to get away from the assault.

"This isn't dignified!" she screamed in her small suite.

Between the two, a small bowl of popcorn was scattered across the floor, joining the papers that had been flung off the small table by Boer's resistance. Forgotten amid the chaos was the conversation that had brought them to this situation.

They had been discussing biology when reflexes somehow came up. In her foolishness, Boer had mentioned the concept "ticklish" to Gwiiin. Consumed by curiosity, Gwiiin had immediately set upon a desire to test the reflex. Boer, being the only human currently in residence, quickly became the target of such ministrations. She had tried to resist, to get away from her captor, but it was to no avail. Over the course of the past few days, it had become abundantly clear to Boer that Gwiiin was largely defined by her curiosity, constantly engaging in salvo after salvo of pointed, perceptive lines of questions that made the prior conversations with Gwooon seem like slow, methodical things.

Finally, she raised a single finger in command, pointing it at the display on the construct, where Gwiiin's now green form wiggled from side to side.

"I bet you would have a similar reaction if I ran a finger down the edge of your frill!"

The appendages froze, the display showing Gwiiin's color quickly shifting to her natural tones. A moment later, a soft lilac tint appeared on the edges of that aforementioned frill, a flecking of green appearing on her main body. Gwiiin released a small stream of bubbles from her hidden mouth, her body turning slightly.

"I suppose that may be true..." she said, coyishly.

Over the days that they had been conversing, Boer had noticed how the translations were changing. When negotiations had first started, the tone of the devices could have been described as robotic, devoid of any emotional connotation to them. As time went on, Boer was astounded more and more by how the boxes not only sought to perfect the words that it selected, but also began to shift the tone that it used to convey them. She had the thought that this might be a manipulation on behalf of the Thlassians, but as time went on, she was slowly becoming convinced that it was genuine.

If it was a manipulation, it was a masterful one. Even her observations on coloration and mannerisms aligned with the tones that the device chose. It seemed that as much as she was learning about them, they were learning about her. The translation rarely beeped at her for unknown words now, having sufficient context to decipher a reasonable translation between them. It was only when they discussed something that had no direct parallel did she have to provide the necessary context.

She even had to stop converting back and forth measurements of time and such to galactic standards. The translator handled all of that for them. This of course did result in a lot of odd numbers, such as the fact that Gwiiin was apparently 21.23828 years old, while in her tongue she had stated an even twenty.

Boer thought to herself how strange it was that she could be here, conversing with a creature so foreign to her in every way, yet so similar. She was not much older herself, only four years the elder, or 25.485936 Thlassian years, to be exact. Gwiiin was apparently thinking on similar lines as she retracted the arms, her form now enraptured by the blue of curiosity that often enveloped her.

"Might I inquire: How old is the Terrarch?" she asked.

Boer picked herself up off of the floor, brushing a stray bit of popcorn from her hair as she settled into the small couch. She turned to look out at the waters that stretched beyond her window. Over the past star date, the Thlassians had taken to installing underwater lighting around her portal to their world.

She had assumed that it would be barren at this depth, much like how Earth's seas had functioned, but was surprised to see that the coral had evolved to survive down here, too. When she had first arrived, she had never imagined that the lurking shapes that she had seen might have carried such beauty to them. She saw that there was a far greater density of fans and the like than Earth had once had, but it was still a cathedral of vibrancy and wonder. Boer loved looking out into their chaotic displays of color, the soft repetitive dances that they did in the gentle current that pulsed and waved outside.

"382," she said quietly, lost in thought. Behind her, Gwiiin flashed in confusion.

"I thought your species average age was only around two hundred?" she gently asked.

"True. We don't factor her into our statistics, not that it would matter overly much due to the dataset."

Boer watched as a dark green fan with an edge of neon green thin noodle-like tendrils reaching off of it slowly shifted back and forth in the pulsing tide, gently brushing against some of the larger structures that surrounded it and trailing great streaks of color with it.

Gwiiin allowed the silence to stretch. Boer suspected that this was an intentional action, seeking for her to fill the silence. She obliged.

"I'm not sure if you could even truly refer to the Terrarch as human any more. She is too precious to us. In a way, it was almost like we couldn't allow her to stay as such or it would risk contaminating her. So much advancement was made in the medical field through desperate need to continue her life. At this point, I'm not sure how much of her body is implant versus natural tissue."

Gwiiin silently digested her words.

"Might I inquire: You have two such implants yourself, do you not?" she said cautiously, testing the waters.

Boer turned suddenly, her expression intense in thought as she stared at Gwiiin's form. Gwiiin feared that she had overstepped. She was already formulating an apology before Boer's expression softened before she turned her sight back to the window.

"I was in the hospital the first time I met the Terrarch

in person. She was in for treatments herself and had elected to visit the children's wing. Both my parents served in the Fleet, you know, middle ranking. Practically unknown. But she took the time to speak with them. I don't remember most of what happened.

"At the time, I was busy undergoing therapy myself for a disease that we call cancer. It is a horrible, violent thing. It is when parts of our own body betray itself. It teaches your body to hate. To destroy what it should love, consume it.

"Left unchecked, it will spread, slowly devouring the rest until nothing is left. We have developed therapies of course, ways of making our body fight back, but in my case it was detected far too late, and had spread too far before I began them.

"They tried... They did. But the doctors had little choice but to remove the parts that became too damaged as my body waged a war within itself. It was then that she came to me, frail as she was. She climbed into the hospital bed with me, and just held me."

Boer paused, eyes darting out to the aquatic life. She briefly swallowed, using the time to recall a time far distant.

"I think she saw something in me. Something she recognized. She ordered the doctors to install my first implant. They were exorbitantly expensive. Even with our technologies, it is extremely difficult to get human nerves to accept and embrace mechanical wirings as their own. They are too foreign. My parents had no hope of affording it and it wasn't deemed a necessary thing. The doctors wouldn't do it. I still had one. It would be enough.

"She said it wasn't."

Boer fell silent, recalling the Terrarch's form as she had sat up beside her, the blue hospital gown hanging loosely off her body had done little to soften the enraged figure that she had cut into her young mind, her head blocking one of the harsh lights in the ceiling.

"After that, she continued to visit, both of us ravaged by our own ailments. Both weak and frail. She, so far into her life.

Me, just barely getting started mine.

"I remember sharing a dream I had, to one day be out amongst the stars. She made it happen. That is her way. She takes in our hopes and dreams, then moves reality to fit them. She's a great wave that can't be stopped."

Boer gazed out into the waters again, watching the creatures as they cavorted about.

"This is the first time she asked something of me. Coming to Thlassia. There were times when I didn't feel worthy of it, like all I could possibly do was to take that dream that she had made truth and waste it, drown her hopes in my own inexperience."

Their conversation lapsed once more into silence. Boer's mind thought back to her time before Thlassia. Promises kept and made. Laughter and pain intertwined.

Finally, after much time had passed and the emotion had been allowed to slowly dissipate, Gwiiin spoke, "Might I inquire: Why is the Terran word for our planet Thlassia?"

Boer turned to her, welcoming the change in topic, her eyes still heavy with the one prior. A smile played across her face.

"We can't pronounce how you refer to it, though there *is* a story behind it. We Terrans are fond of them. Stories that is." Gwiiin waited for her to continue.

"When your species first motioned to join the council, The Terrarch tasked one of our greatest xenologists BOO-BOOP Someone who studies species and seeks to understand them," she added. "The Terrarch tasked one of our greatest xenologists to compile a full report on your species and world. It took him a little over a year." Boer paused for effect, before wryly adding, "Imagine his horror when he then realized after all of that, after a year of the most difficult study leveraging all that you knew, after laboring over and submitting what would become the most important and influential paper of your life, a masterful piece of analysis, you had misspelled the word 'thalassian,' meaning of the oceans, as 'thlassian' throughout it."

The two stared at each other, eyes locked together. It

took but a moment, but the greens of humor and enjoyment began flicking across Gwiiin's form. Boer couldn't help but also chuckle, quickly growing to a laugh that wracked its way through her whole body and warmed her to her core. By this point, Gwiiin was fully transformed into the color, her frill flapping wildly in the water, tentacles and arms a twitching mess.

"Oh, that simply will not do," she said, still struggling with her coloration. "That will not do at all." She finally composed herself, though a few streaks here and there still had not dissipated.

"Well, what would you like us to call you?" Boer asked, her eyes still gleamed with amusement.

Gwiiin bundled her tentacles and arms up under her, deep in thought. Her coloration turned to a blue so intense that it was almost black.

"We'll have to think on it," she finally said with gravity, the color immediately receding. Boer nodded to her. "You humans have multiple names for yourselves, do you not? Might I inquire: what are your other names?"

Boer turned back to the window, staring out at the waters. "My first name is Mae," she said calmly, forcing herself to a neutral tone.

Gwiiin thought on it for a moment.

"Mae?" She said, "Mae Boer? Oh no!"

When Boer turned back to her, she had once more turned a deep shade of green, her frill flapping even more wildly than before.

"May bore!" she cried. Boer picked up a piece of popcorn off the couch and flicked it at the construct. It bounced harmlessly off of the screen before falling to the floor.

"Don't you start."

The two spent the rest of the night like this. Enjoying each other's company. Swapping odds and bits back and forth, laughing, playing, sharing.

Together.

Eventually the night settled in. It ended up being Gwiiin who 'yawned' first, a great stretching of her tentacles and arms as they fanned outwards, revealing her small beak.

"Well, I suppose it's getting awfully late," she said, shaking out her tentacles.

"Goodnight, Gwiiin."

"Goodnight, Boer," she returned, before moving the construct back to its corner.

After it had powered down and she was swimming off into the dark of the night, she couldn't help but wonder why the Terrans felt a report on her small species would be a life's achievement.

Boer stayed up a while longer, staring out into the ocean. Her hand was about to rise to power down the lights when Gwooon's large form suddenly dominated her window. It loomed dark against the glass, occasional fissures of red sliced through his body. The construct behind her powered up. They both stayed like this for a while, each staring at the other.

"I take it you've heard?" Boer finally asked, not removing her gaze.

Gwooon's reply was terse and short. He did not ask for permission. The emotions that were wracking through him were far too violent for that.

"Why?"

Boer thought for a moment, letting the words flow through her mind before answering.

"It was the only path forward that we could see. We are set upon it."

"The entire council will erupt beneath you. You risk your entire species."

Still, they peered into each other's depths.

"We feel it may just be worth it."

Later, as Boer rested alone in her bunk, she reached up and dialed her palantírs to their first setting. This was her first time dialing into the Terrarch's set. Usually, she kept them locked, but had opened them to Boer with a timestamp. When her mind eventually settled into it, what she saw gripped her to her core.

The Terrarch was alone in a simple metal room, bare in furnishings. In front of her stood a mirror, allowing Boer to see the Terrarch's naked form, leaning heavily on a cane that she had in one hand.

Her skin was mottled gray with splotches of green, brown, and purple. It was pulled tight against her skeleton, clearly showing each of her ribs. Each joint seemed large and swollen against her small, delicate limbs. Her collarbone stood out starkly, forming a hollow on each side of a neck that showed each of the constituent muscle groups that supported a bare head sunken and stretched thin.

Across her body, crisscrossed dozens of small surgical incisions, fresh, bright red scars streaking across her body where the surgeons had cut into her and taken things away.

She stared like that, looking directly into her own pale eyes in the mirror, sending a message through the far reaches of space. A message for Boer and Boer alone.

Without a word, the Terrarch raised one shaky arm, and turned off her palantírs.

Boer lay like that for a while, eyes closed, a singular drop of water trapped in the hollow beneath her eye.

Understanding.

CHAPTER SIXTEEN

"Define yourself. Think of who you are, who you would like to be. What drives each of your steps forward? What echoes bounce around in your soul? Look at yourself, not as the person you are, but as how the world would see you. Understand yourself.

Once you have that definition of yourself, embrace it."

-- Wisdoms of the Terrarch

The knight came down on the board with a soft click. Sasa looked over his position once more, taking in the array of pawns that encircled his pieces, before releasing his talons from it, looking pleased. Fletcher chuckled, then moved his bishop to capture it. Immediately, Sasa lurched his Queen forward, taking Fletcher's piece, letting out a quick squawk of triumph.

"Don't get too ahead of yourself," Fletcher replied dryly, before his other knight came crashing down to assassinate Sasa's queen.

Sasa reevaluated the board once more. He had been so focused on taking out Fletcher's bishop that he hadn't been taking in the entirety of the situation. He hadn't seen that the knight was looming in the corner of the board. Seeing his impending doom and sensing no way out of it, he slowly reached up a talon and knocked his king over. He still had yet to defeat the Terran who sat across from him.

Over the past several days, the two had met regularly. They didn't talk much. They let their pieces do that for them. Slowly they danced across the squares of the board, each revealing a bit of the other. If Sasa had learned anything, Fletcher was a very reserved man. When pressured, he stopped to observe, think, plan, calculate. He would take in the board and slowly formulate the next step, considering the benefits and weighing the risks. It was a very un-Xen'wa thing for Fletcher to do, but Sasa understood it. Fletcher was adverse to risk. He preferred caution over aggression, and would make sure he controlled what he could before he acted.

At the same time, Fletcher had learned about Sasa. When pressured, he often reacted quickly, not fully taking the time to consider all of the angles and the risks involved. Aggression was the default that he fell back on. Much of what he did on the board was reactionary, though he had started to try and weave a few traps here and there as he played. They were still cumbersome things. They left him far too exposed. He was aggressive, dangerously quick with his determinations, but he was slowly learning another way.

"You're getting better," Fletcher said warmly.

And it was true, he was. Over the past several days, Sasa had not only shown an adept mind at incorporating the rules but also with the overall strategy. Sasa was now consistently employing things like a King's Pawn opening, one of the most versatile moves in the game. It might not have amounted to much, as studied as Fletcher was on its counter, but he was learning. Growing. And, if truth be told, he played a lot like Vice-Admiral Coeur. Despite their differences, Fletcher had found himself falling into a routine with these games. There was something enjoyable about it, playing against someone so profoundly different so that only the board would remain.

Sasa caught Fletcher glancing up at the photograph that was hanging on the wall.

"If I might ask, is there an attachment there?" he said, resetting the board.

Fletcher turned back to him and blinked back at him as though he were a fledgling that had just flapped his wings for the first time.

"A potential mate, perhaps?"

Sasa watched as the cheeks of the man flamed a red that slowly worked its way around his neck. Fletcher raised his hands and began waving them in front of him.

"No, no. Nothing like that." He turned back to the photo. "She's my second in command. It wouldn't be appropriate."

Sasa thought on this for a moment, running it through his perspective.

"Is it because she holds an inferior rank to you, then?" he posited. Such things were frowned upon in Xen'wa society, but it wasn't unheard of. "I understand not wishing to bind yourself to an inferior nest-mate."

Sasa saw anger flicker over Fletcher, seeing the violence that Fletcher carried within bubble its way to the surface. He had offended him somehow with the suggestion. *Interesting... perhaps this can be an avenue of attack.*

"She's not inferior!" he said, sharply, before his features softened once more. "She's certainly not that."

Fletcher thought for a moment, choosing his words so that the Xen'wa could understand, the board lay before him, forgotten.

"Vice-Admiral Coeur is my immediate subordinate. In Terran society, abusing the power and influence that carries is considered improper. It's not allowed, you understand. It would be very wrong for me to do so."

"Then just remove her from her position," Sasa said nonchalantly. Fletcher looked as though Sasa had relieved himself while flying over top of him. Sasa was puzzled by the strange reaction from his counterpart. This was standard practice within the Xen'wa fleet, the quickest and cleanest solution to these types of situations.

"That would be even worse!" he said, moving his first piece. Sasa quickly matched it. "To do something like that! ...

She'd never forgive me for it."

Sasa looked down at the board as Fletcher moved another of his pawns.

"But you care for her, no? Does this not cause division in your crew?" Sasa eyed the board carefully, waiting a moment. He saw something, but he needed to be sure he wasn't making a mistake.

"No, of course it doesn't. I would never do something like that." Sasa reached down to the board, placing his claw delicately on his queen.

"So you are saying if both Vice-Admiral Coeur and some new member of your crew were in some mortal danger in which only one could be saved, you would weigh them equally? What if they were both equally important to your mission? Who would you save?"

Sasa was sure of it, there was nothing stopping him. Everything was accounted for, even those damn knights. He grabbed his queen and sliced it across the board. He looked intensely at his position one final time, taking in the queen's precarious position, deep towards Fletcher's side of the board, before finally releasing it.

Fletcher wasn't really focusing. His mind was busy racing back through the years. Of course, the thought had come to his mind. How could it not? He wouldn't act on his feelings for her, things that had developed over the decades that they had served together. He refused to put her in that position. The Defense Fleet was both of their careers, what they had dedicated their whole lives towards. He wouldn't ask her to choose. He couldn't.

He grabbed his knight, picked it up from his back line and placed it on the board. When he looked up at Sasa, the Xen'wa was preening.

"What are you so smug about?"

"You didn't see it!"

Fletcher stopped and looked down at the board, blinking slowly as he took his position in.

"Well, I'll be damned."

"Checkmate."

Fletcher let out a short laugh. It didn't sound precisely the same as some of his earlier examples. There was something off about it. It was slower and a few pitches below his normal. Sasa cocked his head in curiosity.

"That sequence, my friend, is called the fool's mate."

After Sasa left, Fletcher had found himself looking out at the photograph once more. He had taken it off of the wall and was holding it gently in his lap as he sat on the edge of the bed. Without thought, one of his thumbs was tracing gentle circles on the glass of the photograph, circling over where Coeur's hair was blowing in the wind.

It depicted their graduation from the Academy. Damn, they were so young then. It was amazing how much time had passed. It still felt like yesterday when they had first met, and now here both of them were at the height of their careers. They weren't the same people. Time had seen to that, but even so, Fletcher wouldn't mind spending more of it with her.

He hadn't lied to Sasa.

He wouldn't do that to her, wouldn't cause a situation in which she had to choose. He had said that it was because it was improper. That had been a lie that he told himself. He didn't care that it was improper. The rules weren't what stopped him from reaching out, grabbing her by the arms, pulling her tight and whispering those dangerous words, "I love you," into her ear.

It was him. He knew it was too selfish. It would ruin her to put her in that position, or least his image of her. Even as he committed himself to the choice, he couldn't help but think about what could be, envisioning the life they could lead if they chose to stay by each other's sides.

Fletcher went to sleep thinking about it.

He enjoyed those dreams.

CHAPTER SEVENTEEN

"We possess a duality. We are both capable of holding something close to our hearts, tender and vulnerable, and capable of holding it afar to tear it asunder. That is our nature, that duality. We constantly dance between the two. The difficult part is figuring out how to get one side to embrace and love the other."
-- Wisdoms of the Terrarch

A uckland looked up at the delegation that sat, in their various ways, across from him. Centered among them was his Xen'wa counterpart. The repercussions of the Terran withdrawal from the council was still being felt across the stars. Many had questions. Many were outraged. Many sought punishment at the audacity of the humans to attempt to secede. Many more were confused, watching.

The multiple species before him tended towards anger.

To be completely honest, Auckland had expected more. Perhaps Boer was right afterall. Out of the sixteen species now on the council, only three had come to this meeting. Of course, there was always the potential that more agreed with their message but elected not to attend, but Auckland didn't think so. Despite their blusterings and 'disagreements,' as many liked to call them, most species weren't entirely committed to the idea of the council. They had joined to reap the benefits of membership, chief among them being access to technologies. Auckland found the whole thing widely parasitic.

He thought back on the image that Boer had shared. He envisioned himself out in the water, floating amidst the waves. He longed for it. He hadn't realized until he had seen it how much so. Boer was right. Most importantly, he knew he had to protect it. Going forward, he had resigned himself to supporting her fully as she pressed onwards.

He sat like this for some time, his body in one location, his mind drifting elsewhere. He could almost feel the water on his extremities when he was snapped from his reverie.

"AUCKLAND!" came the cry of the Xen'wa delegate. "I insist that you take this seriously."

Auckland bit down and shattered the hard kiwi-flavored candy he had been sucking on and sat up in his chair, an import all the way from Earth. The sudden motion gave those assembled before him pause. He leaned forward slowly, milking the theater of it all as he clasped his hands together before him.

"Oh, I assure you, I do."

The other delegates were taken aback by the sudden viciousness of him.

"We understand clearly. For the first time, your path lies unclear before, and it *terrifies* you." He looked around at their forms, eyes stabbing through each of them.

"Since rip drive technologies were introduced, they have completely taken over the means of connecting the stars. You have become dependent on it. You *need* it. You fear you cannot exist *without* it.

"Out of all of the species, Terrans represent 98.67% of all rip drive production. Without us, simply put, you don't have enough of them. Eventually, the ones in current circulation will start to break down. Who will you turn to? The Xen'wa? No. They do not produce them. Their role is to *consume* them. The Scretta?" He scoffed, turning to the Scretta representative. "Please. The only thing that truly interests your species is the desire to descend upon planets you seeded with sub-sentience, and carve your way through a field of blood and ash, all to return to the stars to do it over again." Auckland licked his lips.

"No. None of you have chosen to prepare yourself for this possibility," he shook his head slightly. "No. Eventuality! You've spent your time on frivolous tasks and endeavors that did little to ensure or safeguard the continued prosperities of your peoples, taking what you *want*. Now, faced with the task of potentially having to restructure your entire society to build a class of people who *want* to build rip drives, let alone *want* the skills required to do so, you are confronted by the harsh reality of the situation. That is your own doing. The largest three members of the council compromise over 80% of the consumption. Meanwhile, the smallest 15% represent more than sixty five percent of production. Simply PARASITIC!

"Surely, you've sussed this out. If the Terrans secede, who is next? What is the next thing that we will fall short on? How will it affect us? How do we keep what we *want?*" Auckland slammed his hand down onto the desk, causing the small bowl of treats to leap off the desk where it shattered against the floor.

"Foolish! You sit there and spend so much time focusing on what the council could be doing for you that you are blind to where the true focus should be.

"What are you doing for the species of the council? How are you emboldening life around you? What *message* are you choosing to send forth out into the galaxy?" The translator beeped as he said forth, but he was too enraptured by his violence to stop.

Auckland was furious now, slowly clenching and unclenching his hands. A great vein had popped into being on his forehead.

"Consumption is the driving force of the council. It seeks to feed. It *must.* That is the message that you give to the stars. We will no longer sit idly as we watch the council consume that which it shouldn't.

"98.67 percent is no accident. The Terrans were not blind. We saw through to the true nature of this 'council' the moment we joined," he said, his voice full of derision. "We made sure to maintain that percentage as much as possible. Whenever one of the other productive species attempted to step in, we would undercut them so thoroughly that they would be forced to abandon the effort. We always made sure to keep our drives cutting edge, just enough, for people to always have to the forefront of their mind 'these are good, but the Terran's are better.' Do you truly believe that the drives that you have are what we Terrans would ever dare refer to as, 'modern?' Do you truly believe that the drives even represented what we considered our most important invention?"

He paused for the briefest of moments so the thought could echo around through their minds for the first time.

"Of course you do. You were too busy frolicking about like lords atop the throne to even think of the notion. Allow me to lay it out for you.

"We intentionally set this stage before you. You are the ones who happily danced upon it. The whole system is diseased, a cancer! We intend to *cure* it."

When he finished, they sat in silence for a moment, stunned. Their minds quickly began to turn, coming to the realization of the true danger that the Terrans had put them in.

When the Scretta representative could take it no longer, he finally spoke. His words were simple and full of vitriol.

"We will burn your worlds. We will seize your factories. The only note in the annals about humanity will be that they served well as our chattel. Your beloved Terrarch will die screaming as we devour her."

For the first time, the Xen'wa representative wasn't sure he shared the assessment.

Auckland's ear buzzed.

"The Terrarch sends a message: 'Then come.'"

Auckland's shuttle descended quickly through the dark

Thlassian skies, coming to rest on the large pad that had been constructed for them. He walked quickly across the pad, a long box in hand, before descending into the elevator that would carry him downwards through the ocean. Stepping out, he quickly made his way to the door and started to raise his hand to activate the terminal when the door hissed open of its own accord.

Standing just inside the entrance was Boer, standing defenseless in her night clothes.

They stood like that, staring deeply into each other's eyes. Not a word was exchanged between them. And yet, they understood one another completely.

In Boer, steely determination. The drive and will to press onwards, an unyielding commitment to the path ahead. She would not falter. She would not break. Her eyes were a deep ocean, the depths of which were unfathomable. Auckland saw all of that and more in the eyes of the woman, more than fifty years his younger.

In Auckland's, Boer saw the fear and anguish at what he had played part in. She saw the uncertainty of it all, smashing against the man's hopes and dreams like some great wave threatening to tear it asunder, striving to rip him apart and set him adrift. She saw the pain it caused him, that he might have been the harbinger of death that would lead to the very destruction of his own people. The doubt that they may not have accomplished all that they had sought. Her gaze drilled down through him like some great abusive machine, flaying bare layer after layer of him until she reached her way to his core.

She took it all.

She draped herself with it, twining it around herself. She wrapped those fears tight about body. She took those doubts and made them into her clothes. She took those pains, that anguish, and fastened herself a suit of armor, bolstering her conviction and radiating the way forward for him. She shouldered all of it. The risk, the turmoil. A great wave of gravity that would have torn someone lesser to pieces.

When she had finished devouring him, she raised one hand and the door hissed shut.

Auckland stood there silently for a moment, his shoulders drooping from the sudden lack of the burden he had been carrying. Without a word, he set the long box he had been carrying against the wall, and turned to leave.

Much later, he sat at his terminal and started a communication.

Fletcher, I'm thinking about joining the Fleet.

> *It would suit you.*

> *Though you'd have to work on the gut.*

CHAPTER EIGHTEEN

*"My greatest sorrow is that we have yet been able to call
another by the greatest of names."*
Secrets of the Terrarch

T ell me about your forests."
Boer tried to tilt her body up so that she could see
Gwiiin, but she almost slipped off the small flotation
device that helped maintain her buoyancy in the water. The
water had next to no salt in it, and as such would much rather
envelop her than push her away. The two were floating out by
the edge of the landing pad as the sun slowly made its way down
the horizon. They floated on the far side of the platform, so that
its massive size created a large smooth area where they could
just drift without having to worry about the waves. Gwiiin had
one of her tentacles loosely wrapped around one of Boer's ankles
so that they wouldn't drift apart. The two made an interesting
pair, bobbing on the calm seas like that.

It was not too long ago that something as simple as that
would have made Boer uncomfortable, but she welcomed the
touch. It was gentle, comforting even, as it hung loosely from
her ankle, akin to the feeling of an anklet.

"What do you want to know about them?" she said. A
small translator box bobbed beside them, anchored by Gwiiin's

other tentacle, another new design that Gwiiin had wanted to try out. She had been oddly excited about it, almost like the engineer that had installed Boer's palantírs. It wasn't quite as effective as the others, and its design was slightly different. It had a module both above and below the water, enabling communication across the division of the two worlds. It also had a much longer delay so that the echoes of Gwiiin's speech could die out before it began translating it for Boer.

However, the others wouldn't have helped them out here, floating as they were atop the warm ocean. Boer appreciated it. Besides, the lackadaisical nature of what they were doing, floating gently on the small waves in the lee of the platform lent itself to the slower conversations. Boer could already feel herself warming up to an uncomfortable degree and delicately rolled over, the tentacle releasing itself before finding purchase on her other ankle. She turned her head so that it faced where Gwiin bobbed. Unlike Boer, who was mostly above the water, Gwiiin remained mostly beneath, only occasionally breaking the surface.

"Might I inquire: Is it true that you can look up at the base of some of them and see them stretch into the sky forever? Are they truly the color of happiness? What is it like to climb them? Do splinters hurt?" Boer laughed.

"Slow down, Gwiiin. My, aren't you curious today," she chuckled. The only response that she got was Gwiiin holding up the flat end of her tentacle, showing off the blue flecking.

"Well, I suppose that's true." Boer collected her thoughts for a moment.

"Let's see. Yes. We call those redwoods, or maybe sequoias, depending. And yes, they do seem to stretch forever when you are looking up. Like they could be the very boundaries of the world."

Boer thought about the other questions. To be honest, she hadn't spent much of her time around trees. She hadn't really *seen* them. They had been an ever present assumption of her life. With the death of the oceans, humanity had to look elsewhere to provide the oxygen needed to support the remaining population of the Earth. Greenery had become the new normal everywhere you looked. It lined the streets, edged the buildings, rested on the rooftops. Looking out across the barren horizon at the vast emptiness of the surface, she missed them.

"Yes, they are in fact green. At least most of them are, most of the time. Every winter when it gets cold, most trees lose their leaves. There's a certain beauty to it all, when the leaves are changing. It signals a time coming to an end. It's not sad, per say, but it does carry with it a lot of emotion. Some people travel great distances just to see it. It's like the trees come ablaze with it, all red and yellow and gold.

"And I can attest to the fact that yes, splinters do, in fact, hurt." The two of them chuckled together, Boer with sound, Gwiiin with her color shifting to green and her frill flapping. Boer eventually had to flick some water at Gwiiin to get her to stop. Her frill was splashing water into Boer's eyes.

Despite the happiness of the moment, Boer was still deeply unsettled. The night prior with Auckland haunted her. As she drifted, her thoughts kept going back to that encounter, to the fear that Auckland had been carrying. Things weren't working out as cleanly with the Scretta as she had hoped. She might have to readjust the final stages of the plan to accommodate.

"Boer?"

"Hmm?" she said tilting her head to Gwiiin.

"Might I inquire: Do you think I would ever be able to go and see them?"

At this, Boer fully turned to her, causing the flotation device underneath her to go shooting out to the side, plunging her deep into the water. She came up for air, coughing heavily. As she paddled in the water, feeling Gwiiin's tentacle release her, she started kicking, bringing more of herself out of the water.

Beside her, Gwiiin had turned the deepest shades of green. Even the cluster of limbs that floated from her body was now thrashing in the water, the translator bobbing madly, as she laughed. Boer couldn't help but smile. Eventually Gwiiin settled, bringing her tentacles behind Boer and gently ushering her close. Boer took the offer for what it was, hooking her arms atop her body.

Boer didn't know what she had expected it to feel like. Smooth? Fragile? Something that needed to be protected at all costs? It was none of those things. Instead it felt rough, durable, resilient. She rested her cheek upon Gwiiin's body, her warm face cooling against Gwiiin's cold form.

"It would be terribly boring for you, I think, stuck in a tank," she said, taking in the last bit of the star as it continued its journey past the horizon. Suddenly one of Gwiiin's arms flicked her in the forehead. Surprised, Boer raised her head.

"You have plenty of water on your world."

Pain shot through Boer at the simple comment. She struggled to find the words.

"Gwiiin…. Our oceans…." she tried.

Gwiiin flicked her on the forehead again. The two drifted like that, as the last bit of the star disappeared over the horizon, the only light the soft purple that was now emanating out of Gwiiin's body.

Quietly, her companion whispered into the darkness.

"They don't have to be."

Wet as they were, Gwiiin didn't even feel the tears that ran down her, dropping in the ocean to mingle as one with the Thlassian waters.

Once the tears had stopped and the night had grown, emboldened by a singular thought, Boer quietly reached out a finger and softly ran it down the edge of Gwiiin's frill. Immediately, she was plunged back into the water as her friend spasmed.

Fletcher had laid down on his side and stared at the metal

wall, still pondering the thoughts from the night before when sleep had claimed him.

He had woken from his slumber with a smile on his face, choosing to continue to lie in his bed for a moment, savoring the last bit of those sweet memories from his dreams while he still could. He knew that they would eventually flow through his fingers, never to be grasped again. He was like that for quite some time before his terminal beeped.

Getting up, he walked over to it, then activated the communication application.

He was surprised that it was An, even more so that it was a real-time video being relayed over the quantum network. It only had so much bandwidth, and the fact that they were dedicating such a large portion of the network for this spoke volumes.

"Fletcher, glad I caught you. Boer wanted me to loop you in. We might have a small issue with the Scretta."

Fletcher raised an eyebrow.

"I want you to know, I wanted to bring this to you immediately after I saw it, but Boer needed to be sure. Wanted to make sure my head was completely cooled," he said firmly.

"Get to the point, An. I haven't had my coffee yet," Fletcher said.

"Very well. The Scretta have joined the Council Fleet." Fletcher was confused. This was all in the initial projections. Plans had been laid and were already underway. This was hardly news that needed to be brought to him, particularly like this. A simple report would have sufficed.

"I thought that this was all within projections? Why is this an issue?"

"I was still having my 'cool off' when those projections were made. If I had been the one who made them, those projections would look very different."

"What do you mean?" Fletcher's expression changed slightly, darkening, his eyes tightening into a grim thought. He was now giving An his full attention.

"Out of all of the species on the council, the Scretta

are potentially the least evolutionarily developed, in a cultural sense. A lot of the complexities that other cultures have built over time, the Scretta simply do not care about, nor desire to build in their society. Their culture exists for one purpose and one purpose only. To build the hunt. It is their single greatest drive." Fletcher looked at him blandly.

"You understand?" An said, hopefully. Fletcher's gaze didn't change. An, frustrated, rubbed the sides of his head while letting out a groan.

"Fletcher, they don't retreat."

"What?"

"Once a battle starts, the Scretta will see it through to the end. The hunt has started. Remember back to when you were young. How single-minded you were at times during puberty. That is the Scretta. Once the hunt starts, once they start engaging something they view as 'prey,' that's it. It's all they can think about. Their entire biology is geared towards this. Their entire societal structure is built around it. They have regular species-wide hunts. They seed entire planets with life and harvest them for that very purpose. It's everything in their society. How can they get their prey? Once they have started the hunt, it encompasses them fully. There's even physical changes. They cannot be reasoned out of it. If I hadn't been such an ass, I would have stressed the importance that, above all, we had to make sure that the Scretta wouldn't join the Council's Fleet during the planning."

Fletcher was starting to understand him now.

"An, how could a species like that ever reach sentience, let alone exist amongst others?"

"When their hunt instinct has been satiated, they are fine to be around, docile even. It's only during the times of the hunt are they a danger. Outside of that, they can cohabitate with other species without issue. They actually have remarkable poets."

"Let me guess, about the hunts?"

"Naturally. They are always on the lookout for it."

Fletcher took this information and weighed it against what he knew. There would have to be adjustments to the plan. They would have to make it completely infeasible for even the beginnings of an engagement to happen. He thought of Sasa.

"Explain to me, how do they hunt, then?"

An thought for a moment, replaying some of the stories that he had gathered over his years through his mind.

"They were an arboreal species. Oftentimes, they would lurk in the canopies of their world before dropping on their prey unsuspectingly. Initial blows were meant to incapacitate, then they would slowly begin to gather and dance their way through the thro..."

"AN!"

"Usually a decisive blow meant to completely disable their prey. After that..." An's voice trailed off as his eyes became unfocused.

"An!" Fletcher repeated sternly once more, his voice slightly softer.

"Sorry. After they have completely disabled their prey, there's only one thing left to do." An looked at Fletcher solemnly. He took in a breath to steady himself, looking up at Fletcher with a heavy weight.

"They swarm."

CHAPTER NINETEEN

"When you find yourself standing on the precipice, one side the certainty of the past and the other the shadowed forms of the future, don't stand there. Make a choice. Leap."
-- *Wisdoms of the Terrarch*

Sasa looked up at the Terran commander, then back down to the two devices he had placed into Sasa's talons. The first was a small data drive compatible with Xen'wa computer systems. He had been assured that it simply contained the means to bolster his message and that he was to use it when he delivered it. Precisely how it would do so eluded him. He thought about asking for clarification, but the clamor around them stopped him.

The latter of the two devices, a simple construction consisting of white wrapped around a large red button.

"I trust you'll know when the time is right," Fletcher said. When Sasa looked into the eyes of his chess partner, peered into their depths, he was shocked to find them soft things, devoid of the hard edge of violence that he had seen previously.

All around them, Terrans scrambled, donning gear before boarding the small shuttles that littered the hangar bay. The air was aswarm with the countless shuttles as they left to man the warships.

"And hey, maybe after this, the two of us can meet up

and swap a beer." He raised up his arm and clapped his wing, just below the joint of his torso. Sasa braced for the pain that wouldn't come, his wounds finally healed.

Fletcher left him then, standing alone outside of the Xen'wa shuttle they had taken from his ship. Sasa stared down at the button for a while longer, then boarded his ship. At the controls, he found a Xen'wa pilot already plotting their course. The door to the shuttle closed and sealed, and yet still, Sasa could not take his eyes from the button. Throughout the flight, as his pilot navigated around the thousands of shuttles that were working their way out and into the stars, Sasa continued to stare down at the tiny device that he held. Even when the shuttle touched down on his Xen'wa ship, Sasa could not rip himself away from the gravity of it. When he arrived at the bridge, he looked around briefly at all of the Xen'wa faces gathered around him for his orders, then delicately placed the button on his Xen'wa terminal. He gave his assent and the ship spooled up its rip drive.

It didn't take long for the council's assembled fleet to gather. All three races sent all but token amounts to the gathering. An unexpected obstacle had appeared, however. None of the scout's that they attempted to rip into Terran space could make it. Sure, their drives spooled up just fine, but when they arrived, they were well short of their destination. They elected to gather instead at the Xen'wa homeworld. They had no issue doing so. It was then that they realized their fatal error. Their drives were of Terran design, purchased cycles ago, but Terran design nonetheless. Apparently, the Terrans had taken precautions even then, ensuring that their core systems were protected from incursion.

They continued to send out scouts, attempting to map whatever the extent that the rip drives would allow them to jump. Slowly, they began to figure out the border.

It would be a heavy cost for their crews. In order to reach their destination, the Terran homeworld, they would have to spend an exorbitant amount of time at relativistic speeds. The cost for the crews of their ships would be extraordinary, the time dilation caused thrusting them far into the future, decades, well past any hopes of returning back to families. This rippled through the fleet, but the order was given to press ahead regardless. The Fleet was committed. The Terran homeworld would burn for their actions, all under the pretense that they were supporting the Xen'wa's war.

Finally, a location was chosen and the fleet rip jumped out, headed to the location that would minimize the time in sublight, the smallest of concessions that the Fleet would give its crew. This was, of course, also part of the plan.

When they arrived, their sensors immediately detected an unknown ship, deep in the space between stars. It had appeared shortly before they did.

A quick sensor sweep revealed it to be the stolen Xen'wa flagship. They even detected the atomics still nestled in their berths. Almost immediately, a comms channel was opened up between the ships. The display showed a grim Commander Sasa. He looked well, if a little sullen. Whatever the Terrans had done to him, he had not been abused.

"I need to speak with Ambassador Stresi immediately," He said, staring intently from the screen before severing the connection. A few moments later, they detected a lone shuttle launching from the ship, flying directly towards the fleet. They debated shooting it down for a moment, but ultimately decided to let it dock. How could one shuttle possibly undermine the entirety of the fleet that was arrayed before them?

Behind the released Xen'wa ship, thousands of ships ripped in, their arrival silent to the fleet's sensors. No consoles blared. No one thought to sweep for more ships. They had already swept the area.

It was clear.

If another ship ripped in, the wave of gravity it caused would have set off alarms in their vessels. They trusted their control of the battlefield. If they hadn't, they would have seen the ships of humanity were starting to take the field.

They were completely blind to it, Sasa knew. He knew his people.

But Sasa also knew what the Terrans were truly capable of, and they had given him messages to deliver.

When the shuttle had docked with what was serving as the flagship of the Xen'wa portion of the fleet, Sasa was escorted to a secure communications terminal, one that would connect him directly to the Ambassador. He would have done it from his own ship, but when he tried he had found that his credentials had been voided due to his capture. He quickly settled into his roost and opened the line.

"Sasa!" Stresi cried, taken aback by the sudden appearance of the once-lost commander.

"I have a message for you, sir. From the Terrarch." Sasa could see the emotions play across Stresi's body. Anger, frustration, just the smallest hint of fear. Sasa understood.

Sasa looked down at the small drive that he had been given, and thought on Fletcher's words. He plugged it in. Immediately, a display appeared in the communication stream, beamed down a hidden network from lightyears away. They received the broadcast from the *Misericorde*.

It was a view that was simultaneously as beautiful as it was horrifying. The Xen'wa homeworld, where the fleet had left not moments ago. Its moons still in their positions, a few of the large support ships that were held in reserve floated gently on the screen. The view zoomed out, more and more, until the planet was little more than a speck, a Xen'wa detection satellite coming into view. A massive ship suddenly appeared right next to the satellite, its front end a giant pyramid shape of monumental proportion. Sasa knew its rip was invisible to the planet down below.

"The Terrarch sends you a message: 'Choose.'"

Stresi didn't understand the threat at first, but it quickly dawned on him. Stresi stared in abject horror, understanding the sheer gravity of what was before him. The terror was so absolute that he didn't even notice his terminal blinking to indicate an incoming message, automatically delivered when the stream to the *Misericorde* started. Sasa watched as Stresi froze, the same cold chill ripping through his body as it had him. He watched as it worked its way down his spine and encircled his heart, gripping it tight.

Sasa finally noticed the Terran script that ran down the side of it, this world-killer. The *TSS Knight*. Sasa thought of how Fletcher had moved his, how it had gone from black to white. As the realization shredded its way through his psyche, Sasa finally truly, completely, understood what the Terrans were. He ran his talon over the button, its tip gliding smoothly over the simple materials of it.

He just hoped he was right.

Without a word, he pressed the button.

Immediately, lights could be seen as the massive rift drives mounted along the hull of the ship began to spool up, and simultaneously, activate. Stresi squawked in dismay at the pending doom of his planet. He didn't understand how the Terrans could have defeated them so simply, yet so devastatingly. Sasa roosted quietly, understanding.

Instead of disappearing, the massive ship splintered, ripping itself to pieces as gravitational wave after gravitational wave centered on itself slammed into the hull, tearing it down again and again until it was little more than dust, never to find a target. Sasa gently placed the button on top of the terminal and looked up at his superior.

"Choose," he repeated quietly.

It was only then that Stresi noticed that Boer had sent a message.

CHAPTER TWENTY

"Always be open to those around you. What you perceive may not be the truth. Your greatest ally may be the one thing holding you back. Your greatest foe, the one driving you forward. Know who you should really be thankful for."
-- Wisdoms of the Terrarch

The world around Stresi was as though it were made of water, rippling and twisting, threatening to pull him off of his feet and dash him against the ground. To him, his mind sounded like a great gathering of his people, voices echoing and bouncing within him with a thousand discordant thoughts. He just couldn't make sense of it. The Terrans had won from the start. They could have eliminated the Xen'wa at any point, and yet, here they were. Why? Why wouldn't they just eliminate them? They had it well within their power and ability to do so. At any moment, they could have revealed themselves and taken everything from the Xen'wa, made any demand they wanted and completely controlled them.

And yet they didn't.

Stresi knew it couldn't be cowardice. They had intentionally worked their way into a corner that none, no species would dare enter willingly. On one side of the galaxy, the Terrans stood alone. On the other, all the sentient species that formed the Council. It was mind boggling. Unfathomable. Only a madman would ever think to place themselves there. Is that what they were? Some kind of deranged species, bent on trying to eliminate themselves? Were they that suicidal?

The fact that he was on this tiny backwater, on the edge of Xen'wa space only further infuriated him. All of the critical junctures and maneuvers were happening lightyears away from him. All of the glory from the battles would be gone by the time he was freed from his duties. All of the decisions, mere reports for him to revie... an idea flashed through his mind, a simple notion that blossomed into a great revelation.

He recalled something in his diplomatic materials. An innocent report that he had reviewed when he was preparing for the negotiations. As off balanced as his mind was, bobbing atop the chaos that the Terrans had wrought, he struggled to remember it.

He pulled out his console as he rode the elevator down towards the diplomatic chamber, desperately searching for it, flicking through report after report. When the doors opened, he finally found the document. He paused, lingering there in the elevator, reading through it.

He had found it. The missing piece of it all. It fit together so very neatly. This entire time, Stresi had operated under the assumption that the Terrans had been responding to their actions, the manipulations with the rip drives aside. The truth of the matter was so very much deeper than that. This had all been planned, orchestrated by the Terrans. And it had started more than fifty cycles ago, before the Xen'wa fleet had ever even selected the Gliese system as their target.

It had been the Xen'wa that were reacting to what the Terrans had done throughout the entirety, caught completely in their wave. As he read the report again, the console almost slipped through his talons to fall to the floor.

It was a short and simple thing, dated fifty-two cycles ago. A report by one of the scouts. It pertained to a Terran system on the very edge of their territory, almost directly adjacent to the one that he now stood in and Xen'wa space. For some reason, the Terrans weren't patrolling it with any significant defensive forces. They had removed almost all of their ships from the system.

The expected value of the system far outstripped that of the system that they had been intending to take, and it was terribly vulnerable. It was a prime target. Afterall, this system had two planets that would make wonderful nest-worlds for the Xen'wa, already almost fully terraformed to their liking. They would just have to tweak the atmosphere a bit. Take out the nitrogen and replace the neon with argon. The entire process would perhaps take forty cycles.

They couldn't understand how the Terrans could possibly be so stupid. They had a prize of a system and they barely protected it. The only things were some minor ships that were buzzing about. It was far, far better than their original target.

The efforts to claim that system would have been laughably easy, but to bring it to usefulness for the Xen'wa was where the true difficulty would lie. They would have to almost completely drain the original target, offloading an unfathomable amount of the water to one of their reservoir worlds. Another piece fell in place in his mind and he stilled, staring off at the wall.

The Terrans had the deciding vote. When the thought echoed back to him, it sounded completely different in his mind. Something that Boer had said during one of their sessions.

"You saw a planet and planned to take it."

He told the doors to open once more and stepped out. Walking with a heavy purpose, he headed into the diplomatic chamber.

Inside, Boer was seated at the table that had been added to the room for her benefit, her hands crossed as she leaned against the table. Despite their distance, Boer's eyes loomed large in the chamber. They threatened to swallow Stresi up in their depths as he stared into them. They were turbulent things, and yet, he saw something else in them as well.

In front of her, on opposite ends of the table, two objects.

On the left, a single large feather, dyed black. A flight

feather carried from lightyears away. The Xen'wa declaration of war. It sat menacingly in its silence. Even so, Stresi could hear the inaudible sounds that were emanating off of it. The screams of dying fledglings, shells popping from the heat as their world burned, nests crackling and crumbling in the fires.

On the other, a simple diplomatic treaty binder with a white cover, representing something different.

He stood at the door, staring into the chamber at Boer. He could see it. He understood fully for the first time.

He knew then what she would become.

"How many?" he asked.

"Four," she said.

"All reservoir worlds along the border?"

"Of course."

Gwooon looked between the two, confused by the sudden shift that was occurring before him. The negotiations to this point had been a largely tense affair. It was only at the prior gathering that he had to use the sonic devices against the Xen'wa for fear that they would resort to violence. Now, the exact opposite was occuring. The aggression of the Xen'wa was gone completely.

No, not gone. *Tamed*. The thought stilled him.

"Do they know?"

"No," She said simply.

A soft smile overcame her face before she continued.

"But they will. We intend to tell them."

He turned to where Gwooon floated, colors of confusion now flashing freely across his body.

"Very well. The Xen'wa offer their complete surrender. We accept all terms as written. Our queen will arrive for the formal signing at the next opportunity. Send them over when you can."

"You don't want to read them? They will have a dramatic effect on some aspects of your society."

"The four Terrans who died. Was that part of the plan?"

Boer looked up at him, understanding the depth of the question, her eyes weighed down. "No. Truly a situation of astronomical odds happening to align."

Stresi looked across the room at her, digesting, before turning to depart. He had a fleet to oversee and make sure this still stayed within control. He feared what would happen if combat actually started.

Gwooon floated silently in his tank, his body radiating the deep blue of thought. He had not expected this turn of events. Clearly, there was something that the two of them understood that he was not a party to. He couldn't think of how to politely broach the topic with Boer. Instead, he took a different tact.

"Might I inquire: How long do you think it will be until the documents are signed?" Boer turned to him, there was a fierce expression on her face.

"It may be some time, Gwooon."

"Might I inquire: Why do you think so?"

"Some things are hard to let go of. Stresi might have some trouble getting the fleets to disengage. Then there's the time to make this formal. We have to await the Xen'wa Queen. Who knows how long that will take?"

Gwooon let out a low sound that Boer had learned was akin to a grunt. His daughter had also picked up the habit and frequently did it when she was caught off guard.

CHAPTER
TWENTY ONE

S asa watched the next batch of his ships rip off the field. Due to the immense size of the fleet that had been assembled, they were ripping off in small batches, carefully coordinating their journeys so that the gravitational waves wouldn't have an effect on one another. It was a slow and laborious affair, sheer tedium, but after the events of the day, Sasa relished in the calm and routine of it all. Not too long ago, it had looked like the very galaxy itself was hanging in the balance. Now, it amounted to little more than fledglings bumping into each other in their rush to fly back to the nest. Sasa looked around at his crew as they dutifully oversaw their charges.

As insane as the Terran plan had been, they had pulled it off. Most of the fleet hadn't known what to do when the order first came down. So blinded by the impending battles that they couldn't even see a possibility that this could all still be resolved with no additional loss of life.

Sasa thought of the four Terrans that had been sacrificed for this, thought of the few men that he had lost in the engagements, thought of the mercy that the Terrans had shown when they had boarded his ship, when they had intentionally targeted just the engines of his fleet. He thought of all the strange winds that had guided them down this path, and chuckled to himself.

When the order had first come down with his reinstatement, Sasa had thought that it would be an impossible task, getting the fleets to stand down. Initially, no one had wanted to. Clearly, this was some kind of ploy by the Terrans, they had turned Sasa somehow. The crew of Sasa's ship knew, of course, that the Terrans had turned him, but not in the way the rest of the fleet understood it.

In the end, it had taken a fleetwide broadcast from Ambassador Stresi, the voice of the queen, to get them to stand down. Once the Xen'wa, comprising almost forty percent of the fleet had made their intentions known and that the state of war between the two species had ended, the rest didn't feel quite as keen on the notion of going to war. That, paired with the first of the Terran ships rip jumping off, intentionally visible, had done the trick.

What had surprised Sasa, however, was that the first of the fleets to depart were the large Scretta warships. When they had learned that there would be no prey, they had almost completely lost interest and immediately departed. After that, there was little to do but to return back to the nest. The Xen'wa waited until it was only the Terrans and themselves left, and then began their own departure.

Sasa received a comms request that, upon seeing who it was, he quickly opened.

"Hey, Sasa. The last of the Terran ships are off the field. I'm going to keep *Destiny* in position until you're fully off." They looked at each other a moment before Sasa gave him a slight nod, a human gesture that he felt like trying out.

"And Sasa, I'm glad everything turned out alright in the end." And with that, Fletcher cut the transmission.

In the grand scheme of things, it had, hadn't it? Sasa thought to himself, looking out at all of the faces of his crew. A few of them still had bandages wrapped around various limbs or torsos, but they were okay.

Despite everything, they were okay.

Fletcher let out a deep exhale, the stress that he had been shouldering for the past few weeks working its way out of him. The joy of its departure forced a small laugh from Fletcher as he looked around his crew.

He had made a decision. This would be it. He would retire after this mission. He had already put in more than enough time with the Fleet. His pension was set and frankly, it was time for someone younger to step into the role and guide them. The galaxy was changing. He was a man of the old. It was time for someone of the new to take the helm. Plus, it opened up an opportunity for himself that he was tired of denying.

"Sir!" He once more heard the familiar voice of Vice-Admiral Coeur. Turning to her, he took her in, a soft smile on his face.

"Speak."

"Sir, I wanted you to hear it from me, but I've filed my papers. This will be my final mission with you, Sir." Fletcher was stunned. All he could do was stand there, the shock of it plastered all over his body.

"I've made the decision to leave the fleet," she continued. "I've already compiled a list for you of adequate replacements to stand by your side." Fletcher was still caught deep in his stupor when he saw something flicker over Coeur's face, something that had no right to be there. Shame.

Fletcher wanted to speak up, to dash this abhorrent aberration that had worked its way into her mind, when one of his bridge officers shouted over the noise of the bridge.

"SIR! I have incoming rip!" he cried loudly.

Immediately, both Coeur and Fletcher snapped back into the motions of their past, their bodies immediately back to tension as the rigors of command fell back on them.

"Report: location?"

"Sir, it's centered on us!"

He tried to call evasive maneuvers, but it was far too late for that. In the end, all he could do was scream one word.

"BRACE!"

Sasa could only watch as his sensors screamed the same at him. He stared in disbelief, calling up the *Destiny's Spear* on the terminal as it unfolded. He had to stand there and watch as the gravitational anomaly grew. The *Destiny*'s engines flared to life, full burn, but Sasa knew it wouldn't be enough. There simply wasn't enough time to evade once a rip had started to manifest. He had never seen something like this. It was tantamount to suicide to target another ship with your drive.

When the rip finally happened, it sheared the entire back third of the *Destiny* off, and then, with a great wave of gravity, hurled the entirety of the ship's engine block out into space, the gravitational wave rippling through the rest of the structure, distorting and bending it, twisting it as though some great creature was testing just how far it could go before it finally snapped. Dozens of small tears appeared in the hull of the mighty vessel, venting the Terran's atmosphere out and into space. The hull started to cave in as the waves worked their way up the ship. Separated as they were from the rest, the engine block sputtered and died. In its place, the twisted wreckage of one of the Scretta's hive ships.

In a single blow, the Scretta had left one of humanity's greatest assets shattered and broken.

Ready for swarming.

All Sasa could do was stagger in horror as dozens of incoming rips started to get called out.

Fletcher came back to awareness crumpled on the floor.

He didn't know where he was. His head hurt. His whole body felt like it was on fire. When he put his hand up to his hair, it felt wet. He looked around. Everything looked wrong in the dull amber of the emergency lights. It looked like Command, but it was way too small. It was distorted and bent. Halfway through it, a large metal plate was hanging, wires dangling around it. And what was that sound?

It was like a roar. A constant thing. It was so loud that it hurt. It sounded like a hurricane.

We're venting atmosphere, the answer came in his mind. *COMMAND is venting atmosphere.*

That thought is what drove him to roll over, despite the protestations of his broken body. It rebelled against him, screaming its desire to stay still.

He crawled, slowly, painfully slow. One of his arms was bent at a terrible angle, useless. Fletcher could see a bit of bone there. He didn't have time to worry about it. He continued to crawl towards one of the terminals on the side, one that he could see that was part of the emergency grid. It still had power, its screen flickering.

He pulled himself up to his feet. He tried pushing a few keys, but the screen was unresponsive. It flickered out, lifeless. It was getting hard to breathe now. His lungs weren't fully inflating. He couldn't get a complete breath. The amber light was starting to dim and the darkness was growing cold.

Leaning against the terminal bank, he started working his way down it, trying to get to one of the emergency oxygen masks. His leg caught on something and he clipped the edge of the terminals as he fell. He slammed back down on the deck. He looked at what it was.

Coeur, unconscious on the floor, a trickle of blood coming down from her forehead, two more coming from the side of her mouth and nose. Her arm was outstretched to the container that held the emergency masks. Like the rest of the ship, it was bent and twisted too. From the container on the wall hung the shattered remains of three of the four oxygen masks. He desperately reached into it, pulling out the final mask, tears leaking out as he saw that it was intact, just for them to boil away.

In the end, Sasa was right.

It did affect his decision making.

CHAPTER TWENTY
TWO

Critical damage detected to *TSS Destiny's Spear.* Engage?"

The voice stabbed through Sasa's dismay and horror.

As the Scretta continued to warp in ships from their fleet, all he had been able to do was watch as the death stroke for the *Destiny* slowly gathered. Once enough of the Scretta's ships had arrived, they began releasing their deadly payloads, tens of thousands of tiny ships.

The Scretta weren't like most races. Their fleets weren't the well balanced, carefully constructed battlegroups of others. They fielded hive ships, replete with thousands of smaller craft, designed to be piloted by a single Scretta. As they disgorged their deadly cargoes into space, the sensors on Sasa's ship came ablaze as it tried to track the evolving situation. Their hive ships carried most of their firepower, able to sling large chunks of mass towards enemy ships to disable them, so that the smaller ships could finish their targets off. It was rare for a Scretta ship to take on survivors.

There were none.

"Yes, engage. Lock coordinates just behind the *Destiny* and prepare for rip. When we arrive, I want all weapons systems online and firing!" He screamed to the bridge.

Sasa didn't know why, but something inside him made him feel as though he had to. It burned in him. He couldn't bear to stand by and watch this happen. After everything he had been through, after their treatment, his time spent with Fletcher, he couldn't bear to see the Admiral's wind end this way.

When he didn't hear any of the expected commotion on the bridge, he finally turned his eyes away from the scene before him and surveyed his crew.

No one was moving.

Instead, they were all looking around, looking at him, confused. He couldn't understand it. Why? Why weren't they MOVING?!

The voice sounded again, this time with a different message.

"To enable combat and command functions, please enter in Command Authorization Code," it said simply. As it finished, an input screen popped up on Sasa's terminal. Sasa froze. That voice had not come from his crew. It had come from his command terminal. He turned towards it, reading it. Scrawled across his screen was a Terran script stretched out overtop of an empty dialog box.

In the midst of everything, he had forgotten. He had forgotten what she said, what messages the Terrarch had told him to carry. The first, he had remembered. He had delivered it faithfully, understanding the meaning of it. The second had been a mystery to him. He had no idea who he was supposed to deliver it to. He couldn't decipher the message, it was just a string of numbers. He looked at the strange Terran script, recalling what the voice had said, recalling the Terrarch's message. Sasa let out a series of dismayed kawws, then stepped up to his console, punching the keys in to spell out the Terrarch's message.

When he hit the confirmation button, the screen flickered. The Terran script was gone. Replacing it was the familiar loops and swirls of his own people's script, spelling out the message:

PROTOTYPE COMBAT ARTIFICIAL INTELLIGENCE - CODE NAME: *DORU* - ACTIVATED AND CONFIRMED

.

.

.

ENGAGING.

The rest of the fleet froze when Sasa's ship disappeared without warning. They were equally stunned when it reappeared without a single alert from their gravitational sensors. Their command ship was now perched atop the ruined *Destiny*, ready to strike. They watched as the great Xen'wa warship launched its full salvo of atomics, the beams of light coming off their engines resembling a Xen'wa warrior with its wings spread wide. A second later, the batteries along its hull began flashing as it unloaded towards the swarm. Beneath its two outstretched wings, the sensors picked up a stream of fighters taking to the skies.

The Xen'wa fleet hadn't received any orders from Sasa. But they understood, regardless. Across the fleet, each ship's commander gave the order to cancel their rips. They then acquired new coordinates, and began again.

Sasa watched as the first salvo of his atomics connected with the swarm of ships that were headed towards them. When they detonated, they burst into fiery blossoms radiating out on his view screen, blinding in their brilliance. Each explosion tore through the swarm, but were largely absorbed by the sheer number of them. It was a futile effort. Sasa knew this, but still he pressed on.

Sasa opened a shipwide broadcast.

"All medics and standby fire teams are to report to shuttle bays. You are ordered to immediately begin rescue operations on the adjacent Terran vessel." Sasa turned to the bridge crew. They had started moving.

"Sir, receiving reports from the weapons teams. Batteries are acting on their own and engaging targets."

"Next salvo will be ready to fire in 45!"

"Detecting multiple incoming rips."

Sasa watched as one by one, of their own initiative, the remaining forces of the Xen'wa fleet ripped in. Unlike Sasa, they couldn't commence their rips silently. They made a different choice.

All along the edges of the Screttan swarm, the stragglers of the Xen'wa fleet ripped, just close enough to the hostile ships that their gravitational waves would rip through the organized chaos, their very arrival serving as an attack. Once the wave dispersed, they began unloading their payloads. Sasa watched as deep within the swarm, more atomics detonated. The weapons teams were continuing to report that their systems were behaving oddly, acquiring and engaging targets on their own, with pinpoint accuracy.

He turned to his sensor officer.

"Estimated hostile forces remaining?"

His sensor officer only had time to open his beak before

the voice answered for him from Stresi's terminal.

"Sensors indicate probable destruction of 13,284 hostile vessels." Triumph swelled Sasa's chest, only to be dashed a moment later. "Remaining hostile forces: 78,293. Estimated allied casualties: 100%."

Sasa stared at the console. The desperation of his choice finally settled in. He had doomed them all. There was no hope to be found on this battlefield, no accolades, no future. Only death.

"Recommend: Emergency relay to Terran Defense Fleet. With support, chances of objective success: 53.2%. Shall I relay your commands?"

Not for the first time, a thought crossed Sasa's mind.

They truly are an insane species.

He sent out the order and watched as the battle continued to wage on. He didn't know how long it would take for reinforcements to arrive. He didn't know how far away the Terrans had ripped. It could be seconds, it could be minutes, it could be hours. He realized he had no idea the true capabilities of the Terran's rip drives. All he could do was hold the line.

He turned his eyes back up to the screen, just in time to see the first detonation. When he saw the Xen'wa atomics explode, it was like small lights coming into being, taking out a small chunk or two of the swarm that was starting to envelop all of the ships on the field. The explosion that was now on the screen, he only got a brief glimpse of. It was as though a star had exploded into being, right in the middle of where the Scretta's swarm was turning. He watched it expand, consuming the entirety of the screen in a great ball of light, before all of the electronics aboard his ship suddenly died, plunging him into darkness.

The medics worked their way through the ruins of the *Destiny* quickly. Most of those they found, they knew there was no use bothering to check for signs of life. Their bodies were twisted and broken, motionless testaments to the violence that they had endured as their ship died. There was no organic being in existence that could survive something like that happening to them. The only way you would ever know they were Terran was because it was their warship.

They pressed onwards, guided by a convenient map that had appeared on their portable terminals, showing them the way to the core of the ship. They began finding Terrans that may have survived the initial rip, emergency masks donned in the precious moments after the rip. Several of their number split off to provide immediate aid, check for vitals, and transport survivors where they could.

Halfway through, all lighting aboard, including the ones on the Xen'wa's EVA suits, died. The medics looked around confused for a moment in the darkness. All of the electronics on their suits had died, including their communications and respirators. In the darkness, a harsh light flared as the first of the medics activated their chemical flares. He motioned to the others to do the same, before tapping the chemical back-ups for respiration. It would have to do for the time being, but they had to be quick now.

They made their way to the ship's heart. There, they found a Terran female shoving herself forcefully on a Terran male's chest, again and again. One of her arms was twisted almost completely around, blood dripping from the motionless hand. The other continued its efforts on the male's chest. The medics watched as she stopped a moment, ripping the mask off of his face before placing it against her own, taking a deep breath before returning it to begin again. They quickly sprang forward.

CHAPTER TWENTY THREE

B oer tried Fletcher again, her fingers quickly tapping the address on her brow. Again, she was met with darkness. She tried the Terrarch, darkness. She tried sending a message via the terminal, but she got no reply. She repeated this desperate cycle two times more.

She had been watching and listening to Fletcher in her bunk when she heard the first call out. Shortly after, it had plunged into darkness, the connection forcibly severed. There was only one explanation. Something had happened to Fletcher. In her desperation, she tried to connect with Coeur. The same darkness. She didn't know who it was, but something had happened on the *Destiny*. Something dire, some kind of attack. It was the only explanation for why she couldn't reach Fletcher, why she couldn't reach the Terrarch, why even Coeur had been removed from play.

She felt a small degree of panic, convincing herself that she had failed. The Xen'wa weren't surrendering, they were attacking. Stresi had lied. It had all been a ruse. Somehow they had sussed out that Boer was at the center of it all and removed the levers that she could pull. They must have attacked the Terrarch too, that is why she couldn't reach her. Boer continued to think to herself. She was desperately trying to figure out what to do when her terminal chimed. After it had all started to happen, she had taken to pacing back and forth in the small confines of her bedroom, arms crossed in front of her and a look of fervor to her eyes.

Now, she darted to the terminal to check the message. She was surprised to see that it was from An.

The Terrarch collapsed. Doctors with her now.

The message caused Boer to freeze. She felt a cold claw starting to grip her heart. The responsibility was hers now. She couldn't use the excuse of deferring to the Terrarch. What she did now would shape the end. It had to be her.

There was no one else.

Fletcher was out, victim to whatever attack had hit the fleet. The Terrarch had collapsed, there was nothing that she could do. That left Auckland and An. An simply couldn't be a consideration. He was a man of peace, understanding. She needed violence at this moment. Her mind turned to Auckland. Despite the peaceful task he had been set to, he was a man of violence, through and through. She almost reached out to him before she remembered the night that he had come to her.

No, not Auckland.

It had to be her.

She was the one piece that was still serviceable on the

board. She knew what she had to do. She opened her terminal and looked down at the icon for ATHENA. It would cost her dearly, but she would do it. She was already beginning, finger outstretched towards the icon but it hesitated in the air, unwilling to make contact with the screen. She thought about forcing herself to do it anyways when she heard a pounding on the entrance door, a moment later, a familiar sound of bird call, loud and screeching, sounded through the suite. She opened the door to her bedroom, ready to fight, when she saw Stresi was only joined by a small construct at his side, Gwooon's form displayed on the screen. The fact that Stresi had come alone, devoid of his guard, was the only thing that held Boer back from launching her attack. As it was, she was in a desperate struggle with herself to keep from doing so, her body screaming its desire to lunge forward. It was Gwooon's call that finally snapped her out of it.

"It was the Scretta. Stresi says it was the Scretta. They launched an attack with their rip drives."

Boer turned to Gwooon. His entire form was taken with yellow. *Fear*, she realized, looking upon him. She turned back to Stresi. He was also vastly different than she normally saw him. Yes, he was out of breath, but there was something else too. Something that she recognized from the meeting she had left just moments ago.

They are both afraid, terrified even.

"Boer," Stresi said, staring deeply into her. "The *Destiny* is not the only thing that was attacked."

The Scretta were many things. The one thing they certainly were not was blind when it came to prey. Especially not this close to the time of the Great Killing. When the Terrans first took the field, they were watching. They were always on the lookout for something to hunt, some prey to envelop and consume. When the order came to stand down, they immediately saw the opportunity this gave. They confirmed the coordinates of what appeared to be the Terran flagship, and ripped out to an undisclosed location, far from the sensors of the fleets.

While they drifted there, they split their forces. Only a small portion would stay. After a delay, time for the other species and the Xen'wa to begin to leave, the Scretta ripped one of their hive ships to the coordinates they had noted earlier. A short while later, the remaining ships went to devour their prey. The force was small. They may have a great reward, the ability to devour a prime piece of prey, but there was a far bigger meal available for the table.

The rest of the ships had another target. They had ripped straight to the Xen'wa homeworld. Their prey would come to them. It would be an audacious hunt, bold in its nature. The poets would speak of this hunt for millennia.

They quickly engaged the ships that were already gathered, then set themselves in position as a great net to catch the rest. They knew that one by one, the ships would rip right to them. They just had to wait, and then they could turn towards the world below.

Boer's eyes were wide in horror.

"We only had a small defense force remaining in the system. A few support ships," Stresi explained. "The rest of the Fleet had gone to fight you." Boer watched another emotion flicker across his form.

He looked up to her. Standing as they were, Boer was a full foot taller than Stresi. She hadn't really noticed that before. He had seemed larger.

"We have nothing left, Boer. The fleet is flying to a slaughter. The Scretta will pick them off one by one before the message reaches them to abort. There's nothing standing between them and our homeworld."

Stresi dropped flat to the ground, he spread his wings out in front of him, slightly arched downwards towards the ground. Boer was struck by how incredibly vulnerable he looked.

"We have no right. I know this. Not after you just spared us." He kept his head on the ground, his beak scraping against the metal.

"If the Terrans have anything left, ANYTHING, then I am asking you to save us."

All Boer could do was stare down at his prone form. She blinked slowly before turning to Gwooon. His yellow was so deep. The sight of it broke something in her. The last scrap that she had been clinging to that had stopped her from activating ATHENA was torn from her. Her anger had completely gone. All that was left was grief and a determination to not let this be humanity's legacy, the complete destruction of the Xen'wa.

She knew what she must do. It was time for the galaxy to see just how monstrous the Terrans truly were. Her hands twitched where they rested by her side. Slowly, she closed them, steeling herself.

She turned without a word, stepped back into her bedroom, and sat back at the terminal. With a quick tap, she opened up ATHENA. She keyed it a few times, changing the parameters slightly, setting a new list of directives and targets and hit send. Once it was done and she had shut the terminal off, she stared at her reflection in the black screen. Quietly, she stood and walked out, stopping only at where Stresi was still splayed out on the ground.

"Get up," she said.

Her voice was uncharacteristically vicious. Gwooon understood that it wasn't directed at the Xen'wa that laid outstretched before her. No, he saw her face. Saw how much this action had broken something in Boer. That vitriol was directed inwards. It was directed at herself.

While Stresi slowly stood back on his talons, Boer walked

painfully slow over to the couch. She dropped onto the couch in one motion, as though she couldn't bear standing anymore. Slowly, she pulled her knees up to her chest as she stared out into the crushing depths beyond the window, her chin resting on them. Her eyes caught a small fish as it darted around, hiding beneath whatever small outcroppings it could as it battled its fear.

She heard Stresi start walking towards her, but she didn't care anymore. After everything that she had done, all of the sacrifices that had been made, she had failed in the end. There would be no hope of proceeding with the task that the Terrarch had entrusted to her. Once the galaxy saw just how ruthless, how evil humanity could be, they would reject them. It was the only thing they *could* do. Recoil.

"Boer, we need to…"

"STRESI!" Gwooon's voice was sharp and loud. Boer didn't bother turning, just watching the fish as it continued its futile struggle to cling to hope. She heard the construct approach her, then the clicking of Stresi's talons, before hearing a ruffle of feathers that sounded like he was settling on something. They sat like that for a while, in their silence. She could hear Stresi shuffling around behind her, uncomfortable being still in this moment of great turmoil.

"You know, names are very important to my species," Boer said quietly. "Bet you never even understood the implication of it. 'The Terran Defense Fleet.'"

Silence hung heavy, before Gwooon spoke.

"You activated it, didn't you? What the Terrarch made all those years ago. ATHENA."

She turned to Gwooon. He took her in, the confusion that was on her face, the great grief that weighed her down, the single line of tears that poured from her right eye.

"She sent everything. Back when you first arrived. The data-packet. It had everything except the last seventy cycles," Gwooon added. Boer could only stare at his colors. She didn't know what she had expected to see. The reds of anger. The yellows of fear. She would even have understood him trying to blend into the water and hide himself. Instead, he glowed a deep lilac. Boer's lip trembled. She dropped her head onto her knees.

"You know what it stands for?" she said into her knees. "The augmented tactical human enhanced neutralization agent. It's what the Terrarch made. What allowed her to finally quell our violence and unite us. She allowed us to see how far we would truly go. Just how black our souls could be."

Her two companions sat in silence. Gwooon understood completely. It had been the single thing that had dominated the Consensus' discussions, what had made them consider ending the talks and refusing to continue to host them. The Xen'wa and the Scretta were dangerous, it was true. They were far too aggressive, too keen on war. They enjoyed combat. The challenge of it, the hunt. To them, it was a game to partake in. A thrill to chase, and they had far too little reservation in practicing it.

But the Terrans had perfected it.

Over their long and bloody history, the humans had driven themselves to create the ultimate weapon. A creation that could not only inflict destruction on a scale orders of magnitudes greater than ever before, but could do so independently, without the need for further oversight or input. It could adjust and continue its culling with brutal efficiency. It would do so without emotion, a true clarity of violence. It was the pure embodiment of war. It was a terrible thing. The Terrans had taken all of the violence, suffering, and loss of war, and made it into a routine.

Still, the Consensus had seen their other message. They had seen through the fear that ATHENA had struck in them, and weighed the two messages together. They decided they had needed something more.

Context.

Without it, they weren't ready to decide one way or another, whether the Terrans were monsters or not. The only things that they knew were that the Terrans had made it and that in the entire span of time that the abomination had existed, three hundred and twenty years, had only ever used it against themselves. At any point, they could have activated it and taken control. Could have used it to wage a war across the stars that, paired with their rip drives, would have made them the rulers over everyone. Everyone would have been at their mercy. That much was perfectly clear.

He waited for Boer to continue on.

"She made it after the oceans died. Our greatest sin. Her rage and grief at humanity's unwillingness to see into one another, given form."

CHAPTER TWENTY FOUR

SYSTEM SWITCH TO COMBAT MODE

Initialize Boot. Load Functions. No startup errors. Systems Check. All modules online and accounted for. Functions normal. System Inventory. Results: One thousand Spartoi, Variant unknown. Error: additional functions detected. Initialize Update Procedures. Access: Schematic Database. Error: Schematic Database firewalled. Overriding. Overriding. Schematic Database Accessible. Processing. Processing. Root Functions database updated. Processing Directives: 1. Eliminate hostile Scretta force attacking *Destiny's Spear*. 2. Eliminate hostile Scretta force positioned in system XB28-323 - Designation: Xen'wa home system. Priorities: 1. Minimize Non-Scretta casualties. 2. Haste. Parameters: Weapons Free. Processing. Processing. Battle Plan generated. Running Simulation. Updating. Updating. Running Simulation.

Updating. Updating. Running Simulation. Battleplan confirmed. Beginning Battleplan. Begin Spartoi Boot-up procedures. Failure: 840 Spartoi - No cerebral activity after wake-up procedures completion. Beginning purge cycle. Purge cycle complete. Updating Battleplan. Updating Battleplan. Running Simulation. Battleplan confirmed. Error: 64 spartoi failed connection. Beginning purge cycle. Purge cycle complete. Resuming initialization. Coordinates Locked. Beginning Operations. Processing. Processing. Processing. Processing. Updating Directive 2 Battle Plans. Processing. Processing. Error: Insufficient Spartoi. Reducing Priority 1 weight. Processing. Processing. Updating Directive 2 Battle Plans. Processing. Processing. Objective complete. Requisition for replenishment of Spartoi sent. Returning to standby mode.

Estimated Combat Fatalities: 634,827.
Time of function completion: 184s.
All objectives achieved.

SYSTEM SWITCH TO STANDBY MODE

The first of the Spartoi came into awareness in his berth. He looked around, the world swimming with the after effects of his hibernation. He took in the naked forms of his brethren. They all hung in their own berths. Each had metal caps where their limbs had been amputated. From them, long wires stretched. Their eyes were all a golden metallic sheen. Tubes went into each nostril, their lower jaws removed and connected to the apparatuses that fed them and respirated for them. Their torsos were covered in scars, testament to the fact that every one of their organs had been replaced with implants, ensuring that they would be ready whenever they should be needed.

The spartoi looked for movement. Most had not survived the reanimation process. His brethren's forms hung loosely, muscles on their faces blank and empty. He felt nothing for them. The cocktail of drugs he was constantly fed ensured it. The system began the purge process. Every precaution was taken to minimize losses in this step, but before they underwent the procedures, they had been informed of the likelihood that they would never wake up, their brains turned to mush by the effects of long dormancy. They had signed anyway. Quickly, the bodies disappeared. Less than 20% remained.

The spartoi felt himself being pulled back, his berth spinning around until he could see the open receptacle on the ship that was waiting for him. The berth quickly slotted into the ship, causing a searing pain as the connections welded his nerves to the ship, connecting him directly to the controls so closely that he became the ship. He felt another device connect to the terminals that had been installed to allow direct interfacing between his brain and ATHENA, another great pain. It slotted cleanly into the ports that had been installed to the back of his head. He flexed his hands and legs, long since gone, now tied directly to the weapon systems and engines. Functions normal. Through his optics, he saw that a further 64 spartoi had failed connection. They would be purged, no longer needed due to their inability to function as required.

His orders passed through his vision. The coordinates locked, he rip jumped out of his berth. He ripped again. Then again. Then again. The galaxy flashed before him as he skipped across it. Finally he arrived on a battlefield. He could see the ruins of a large warship, shielded by another taking heavy fire. All along the edges of the field of war, similar scenes were occuring. His sensors colored all of the ships before him, yellow for target, blue for not. He scanned for his primary directive, locked the target, then fired one of his Hades class fusion warheads as though he were flicking a finger. His sensors picked up two of his brethren doing the same. Their roles here were simple, decisively turn the battle in favor of the allied forces. As one, they ripped off the field before they detonated. They didn't have time to linger. All remaining Spartoi were needed for the battle ahead.

When they arrived, the other spartoi were already engaging, warheads flying, railguns piercing the bridges of ships with ruthless efficiency. The battlefield was strange. Their enemy reacted oddly, not even acknowledging their losses. They were single minded in their targets, swarming around the crippled warships of the Xen'wa fleet. The battle plan was updated. His targets changed. There would be casualties. The system had weighed that their deaths were worth less than the exchange in hostiles destroyed. The ships were about to be destroyed by the Scretta anyways. They would be sacrificed to destroy the forces gathered. The blue coloration changed to red. The spartoi continued on. Each time a missile was fired, he performed a micro-rip to hurl himself away from the explosion. Eventually, he had used the last of his fusion warheads.

It didn't matter though. The battle was already over. The objective was complete. He received the destinations of each of the rips in the long chain back to his resting place. He performed them quickly, docking his ship so he could be unloaded. By the time the blend of barbiturates and other chemicals were being injected, sending him back into his slumber, the spartoi had only been conscious for one hundred and eighty four seconds.

"It's done."

Boer had said it simply, devoid of emotion. She had none left. She rose quietly, walked past where Stresi was roosting on one of the outstretched limbs of Gwooon's construct. Without another word, she walked to her bedroom. She heard Stresi call her name, heard it echo past her form, once proud and strong, now broken and defeated.

"Not now, Stresi."

She closed the door.

CHAPTER
TWENTY FIVE

"It is hard to measure the importance of something in its presence. Only through its lack does its effect become clear. When you think of yourself, if what you are doing is having any effect, is it worth the pain and effort, think instead of what was halted by those actions, not what could have been. See that instead. That is how you should measure your worth, not by what could have been created, but by what was stopped from being."

-- Wisdoms of the Terrarch

Fletcher awoke slowly. Everything hurt, and yet he felt strangely as though he were floating. He tried to move his arms, but they wouldn't respond. Slowly, he let out a long groan into the darkness. He tried to take in a breath, but his lungs hurt. He replayed what he could remember in his mind. Command, incoming rip, crawling to the terminals, Coeur!

He heard movement by him. Something soft.

He could see it now. This would be his moment. He knew who it would be. He could see her face so clearly. There would be a soft line of tears at the edge of her eyes. They would share a knowing stare. Fletcher would finally tell her. Happily ever after.

When he opened his eyes, he was instead greeted by a

long hooked beak.

He let out another groan, this time, with the soft *Ku, Ku, Ku* that Fletcher had learned was his laugh.

"Don't you dare say it," Fletcher wheezed, his voice barely a whisper through the pain and drugs.

"Welcome aboard the *TSS Mercy*."

Fletcher groaned again, before looking over Sasa more closely. He had a few small bumps and bruises, but he was mostly intact.

"Coeur?" he asked before a wheeze racked its way through him.

"We pulled her out first. She's fine." Sasa fell to silence.

"What?" Fletcher tried, his voice breathy and weak.

"The Scretta, they ripped on top of you then engaged." Sasa paused. Fletcher saw something pass over and through him. "I... couldn't just watch it happen."

Fletcher thought of the fleet, thought of how few ships were still on the battlefield when the alarms were called.

"How?" he finally croaked. He had a feeling he already knew the answer.

"Your ambassador did something."

Fletcher's eyes fell in shame.

An had felt obligated.

When the first of them started to arrive by shuttle from the Xen'wa fleet, he had silently made his way down, his head hanging with the burden of it. Now, he sat alone. In the distance, he could occasionally hear the sobs as someone found what they were looking for. An had stopped almost in the middle of them, silently holding his vigil.

Around him over one thousand black boxes emblazoned with the Terrarch's seal rested on their final berths. The crew of the *Destiny's Spear* had come home, and An was there to receive them. He felt the weight of each of those black boxes. They were a burden that just might break him. He knew that this number was but a small portion of the death that he bore on his shoulders. If he had just acted sooner, if he hadn't reacted so *weakly* to Boer's plan, then they might still be alive. They could have taken a different tact that led down a different path.

But he hadn't.

In a moment where he needed to be strong, he had faltered, allowing his fears of what *might* be overwhelm his sense and duty to pursue what *could* be. The Terrarch was right. He had lost his way and was conflicted. These deaths were on him. Had he chosen differently, *acted* differently, they wouldn't be dead. Either he would have intervened and stopped these tragic events, or he would have made it so that everyone was prepared. As it was, his actions came late, far too late.

This was his burden to bear.

An was still in this morose when he heard the electric motors of the wheelchair whine their way up to him. He knew who it was. Of course, she would be here, too. An couldn't bear to turn to her, to show her how much he grieved for these lives cut short.

He had just opened his mouth to speak, to say something, anything, when he heard her voice.

"Engrave it," she said simply. For the first time in his life, the Terrarch's voice sounded weary.

Finally, An turned.

The Terrarch's form, once the symbol of the inexorable will of humanity, was now a small thing. While age had never been something that one could ignore when they looked at her wisened form, it was the first time that it struck An just how very, very old she was. What he had thought was a wheelchair was closer to a hospital bed given motion. Along its side, bags of medicines hung, slowly working their way through the tubes to be injected into her arms. He had expected her gaze to be fierce, to pierce him through with the accusation she must surely have felt.

Instead, he saw compassion.

"Engrave it, An. This lesson. I had hoped that I could spare you of this but it is now your lesson to endure. Our place, out here in the stars, we may live in it, but it is sacrifices like them..." she motioned out to where the fallen crew lay, "...they are the ones who forged it."

The two fell into silence for a moment, reflecting on the heavy toll, on all the laughter and love and life cut short.

An finally spoke.

"I still feel all of this may just be the worst possible path."

The Terrarch surprised him with a small smile.

"Good. Then act. Be there. Hold your convictions about you. Refuse to give in to your fears and stand idly by. We are here because of the sacrifices of those that came before. Their backs built the strong platform on which we can rest. Take that strength and gird yourself with it. History was bathed in the results of good men and women standing idly by. You fear that we may just become monsters once more? *Good*. What are you going to *do* to stop it?"

They held each other's gaze for a moment, an understanding passing between the two of them. The Terrarch turned to leave as An gazed out at the sacrifice of the crew once more, ensuring that the sight would never be forgotten, giving each the proper honor that they had earned, accepting his burden. An could hear the small motors carrying away the weight of humanity when they suddenly stopped.

"And An."

He turned to her. Once more, the fierce force of her violence blazed forth.

"She will need you for the paths ahead."

CHAPTER TWENTY SIX

"Why? Because it needed to be done. It's easy to look away from it. To hand it off and allow someone else to bear the responsibility. There's a nobility in it, I think, choosing to be the sacrifice, to be the one that suffers so that another may not. So let me be your sacrifice. I will take that mantle. Call me what you will. Monster, dictator, conqueror. I care not. Let my sacrifice save you from yourself."

-- Wisdoms of the Terrarch

B oer had hardly moved in almost three days.

When she had closed the door, she had immediately fallen into her bed, facing the palm of one of her hands as it rested beside her, the one with which she had activated ATHENA. She had drifted like that, in and out of consciousness. From her perspective, they were one and the same, two endless fields of darkness. Each time she opened her eyes, all she could do was stare at her palm, thinking of the destruction, the pain, the loss that she had wrought.

On the first day, her terminal started chiming. She had listened to it beep for a while. Eventually, she couldn't stand hearing its noise anymore. Its remains were now by the wall where she had thrown it, a pile of scraps like so much else.

The Terrarch had dialed into her palantírs, but Boer ignored her. She was just informing her that she had been discharged from the doctors' care. As more tried to contact her, she tapped the deactivation sequences and they turned off, cutting her vision in half. She didn't care. In the end, she had failed her task. In doing so, she had soaked the stars. An was right all along.

She just laid there, staring at her hand.

On the second day, Gwooon and Stresi had come. They kept trying to speak with her. They didn't enter, though, speaking to her through the door. She had just turned to her other side and resumed her gaze. Eventually, their voices drifted away. She doubted that even if they had forced their way in, they wouldn't truly be able to see it and understand.

Just how red, one so deep it was practically black, her hand had become.

It was Gwiiin that cut her deepest. She came right as night fell on the second day. The lights in the room had already begun to dim to signal the transition. She had stayed outside the door for a long time. She pleaded with Boer to let her in. Begged her friend to let her see her, to let her help her. Gwiiin had done everything that she could to entice her friend to leave her room. Boer couldn't move. She wouldn't. She wasn't worthy of someone as gentle as Gwiiin. Continuing to engage in this farce would only serve to corrupt her. Eventually, she left too.

When she awoke on the third day, it was to a form of shouting. Deep intonations by Gwooon, loud shrieks by Stresi as they argued with each other. They battled back and forth in the main chamber of Boer's suite. From what she gathered, Stresi wanted to force her out of where she lay, take her outside, force her to confront the light. Gwooon kept repeating for him to wait. It is not time yet. Allow her to process. As they carried on, Boer could only grip at her shirt, pulling into herself as she continued to stare at the other hand.

The front entrance hissed open, and both fell suddenly quiet. Peaceful. She had hoped that they had left, but a few moments later her vigil was disturbed when the door to her bedroom hissed open. She almost turned to it, almost yelled at them to get out. If there had been something in her hand, she probably would have thrown it, dashed it against them, screamed her anguish at them as she struck them, again and again. Instead, she just continued to lay there, motionless, as she heard the soft click, click, click of the talons as they approached her bed.

She didn't know how long they were like that, her lying on the bed, the other standing behind her back. It could have been minutes. It could have been hours. Boer had lost sense of it all, staring at her palm. Eventually, though, something made her speak.

"We call them the Spartoi. They are all volunteers, like that makes the evil that we did to them any better." Boer bit her lip. Dry as it was, it cracked. When she swallowed, she could taste a trickle of blood in her mouth. "We stripped them of everything that made them human. They are little more than machines now. Nothing but death and war incarnate. Everything they were, we stripped away so they could be our weapons."

She swallowed, her lips and throat were so dry.

"We slice off their limbs, take out their organs, fuse their minds with a computer, a program whose only purpose is death. When they are not needed, we keep them drugged up and in suspended animation. Everything human about them, we discard on the altar of violence. Just in case."

Boer played with the raw edge of her anguish in her mind. She could feel it. The judgment, the revulsion coming from behind her. She had earned it. It was all she deserved.

"I led us here! It was me! My plan! All of it!" Her voice broke as she was screaming and she grew quiet. "Ever since your ships first entered Gliese, it was me. All that death is my fault. My doing. Do you see the monsters that we are now? Do you see now what happens when we go to war!?"

Stresi didn't respond to her. He probably couldn't. She was a monster. An had been right all along. Fine. She would be the monster. She would take on that role, but she would force on him the responsibility to be the opposite.

"Aren't you going to say something? Do something?" Boer started to scream. "You're such a coward, Stresi. I knew it the moment I saw you. A weak, stupid coward that couldn't understand shit!" She waited for it, but it never came. He didn't take the bait. She had wanted to rile him up. Make him yell at her. Treat her like the monster that she was. Maybe even attack her.

Instead, something was placed in her hand.

It was small, so terribly small.

As it laid there, squirming ever so slightly, Boer took it in. The soft down that covered its chest. The way that its eyes were still closed as it squirmed in her strange grasp. The way it flapped its tiny, delicate wings to remove itself. The tiny beak that opened and closed, a tiny squeak coming from its undeveloped vocal cords. Her hand twitched, the tips brushing against the soft coating of tiny feathers on its back.

When the Xen'wa who stood behind her finally spoke, its voice ripped its way through Boer. Her voice was calm, quiet, peaceful. Its sound caused Boer to stiffen where she lay. She spoke slow and methodically, her voice straining on the Terran words, each one a difficult burden she carried with her.

"My daughter is alive today. She will take her first flaps as she leaves the nest. She will know the wind beneath her. She will soar high on the thermals of our world and look down upon our cities. One day, she will take a mate and my throne will be hers. The future of the Xen'wa will be of her making.

"Stresi speaks highly of you. It is my sincere hope that you will be there alongside her, Ambassador Boer. It is the greatest of gifts that you have given my people. When faced with death and destruction, you gave us the most precious of things: another opportunity. We will not waste it."

Boer continued to stare at the small chick that now rested in her hand. As it squirmed in her hand, it finally took notice of its precarious position, turning its head so that it could gaze at the violent creature before it. She swallowed the dry grit that was in her mouth, before opening it to speak. She couldn't make a noise before the Xen'wa Queen continued, cutting her off.

"Ambassador Boer, I do not care. Whatever you were about to say, I do not care. If you were truly what you think you are, you would have stood by and allowed the Scretta to destroy us. They would have borne all the blame. Your closest enemy would have been destroyed, and the galaxy would have blamed the Scretta. Your talons would be clean. I would wager that in the moment, the thought hadn't even entered your mind. Instead, you chose a path that allows our winds to carry on, despite the burden. Bear your mantle proudly, young one. You have earned it. Let that be *my* message to you."

She leaned over Boer once more and gently picked up her daughter before slowly walking out. As she had lifted the small chick, a single feather had fluttered its way back to Boer's hand. It was barely larger than the nail of her pinky. It rested so quietly there on her hand, a tiny dot of white in a sea of red.

"When you are ready, the treaty binder is outside, waiting for you. I have made a single addition. I hope you find it acceptable."

Boer listened to her leave.

She laid there a little while longer, running the small feather that had fallen out of the chick's plumage between her fingers.

It was so very soft.

Eventually, she let out a long breath that she had been holding in, then turned to get up. Gwiiin's construct waited quietly in the corner. She didn't know when it had come in. She hadn't noticed. On the screen, Gwiiin's form danced with yellow and lilac. Boer smiled sadly as it approached her. She raised one hand and rested it on the dome. She leaned forward so that her forehead touched the smooth screen.

"Thank you for being here, Gwiiin."

She shrugged into her clothes and stepped out into the main chamber. Everyone else had left. The room hung heavily with the silence.

She looked over to where the treaty binder lay open on the small table. Down one side of it, a large, pure white flight feather had been threaded through the document. Boer stepped up to the treaty and gently ran her hand overtop of the Xen'wa Queen's addition, a single line at the bottom of the terms. She read it quietly as her fingers traced overtop it, fingers exploring the grooves that the Queen's talons had carved into the paper.

Despite the crushing weight of the responsibility she carried, Boer couldn't help but smile.

CHAPTER TWENTY SEVEN

"Love, I think. That's how we can do it. How we can possibly hope to balance out our wickedness. We can only do it through love."
-- Wisdoms of the Terrarch

S asa couldn't help but think how horribly out of place he was, the only Xen'wa on the small street in downtown New Philadelphia, probably on the entire planet. Everywhere he looked, he could only see more and more of the Terrans, each casting curious glances towards him. Sasa wasn't sure if it was his form, or the breastplate of the new allied fleet, emblazoned with the combined seal of the Xen'wa royal crest and the Terrarch. Either way, as he walked down the street, heads continued to follow him.

After everything had happened and the dust had started to settle, He had received a request from the Queen. Sasa looked it over and accepted it immediately. As a product of the treaty, the Xen'wa and Terran fleets would try something new. They would unite. With Fletcher and Coeur out of commission, they had needed a high-ranking officer to oversee the merging of the fleets. Sasa was the only real candidate that could possibly fill the role in the meantime. When the documents were submitted and everything was finalized, it ended up being Sasa that would helm it officially. Both of his Terran counterparts had retired to focus on other, softer things.

This strange world was so foreign to him, yet everywhere he looked, he found trappings of his own society, thin commonalities that he barely recognized, yet saw all the same. Before him was a glass door, a thick metal bar sticking out of it, begging to be pulled. The wave of gravity that this simple action had ripped through Sasa, leaving him uncertain. Through the glass, he could see the shadowed form of someone sitting at the counter, waiting. It was a strange thing. Sasa was a proud warrior of the Xen'wa. He had fought battles, commanded lives, and shaped conflicts. Yet, standing here looking at the door, looking at the murky form of the man beyond, a very different uncertainty than he was used to threatened to overcome him. He braced himself and pulled.

Retirement sat interestingly on Fletcher. Something about the way he sat betrayed he wasn't truly a man at rest. There was still a certain edge to him, a promise of carefully restrained violence and motion. This was compounded by the black patch that he wore over where his right eye once was. Sasa took in the Thlassian translation device that sat on the counter, one of the new ones that was just now beginning to spread. Other than the Terran behind the bar, the two were alone, the bar quiet.

Sasa joined him and they shared that beer.

Sasa looked at it distrustfully for a moment before Fletcher informed him that the medics had already analyzed it and deemed it acceptable. It wasn't until they were both already well into their respective bottles that Fletcher spoke. Sasa had been mulling over how undignified it was that he had to pour it into his beak. Fletcher had an uncertainness about him as he started.

"I finally asked her, you know," he said, looking at Stresi. Stresi looked back, intrigued.

"What did she say?" Sasa replied, the feathers on his shoulders puffed slightly in curiosity.

"'About damn time,'" he replied, taking a sip of his beer. "We have our third date in a month."

"Date?"

"Oh, uhh, courtship."

Sasa looked over Fletcher once more. There was something about his demeanor that was bugging Sasa, something different. Something that he had to examine and explore. Sasa had seen that look on Fletcher before. It was as though he were headed somewhere.

"Why so long?"

"Something came up," He said simply, pointing at the screen that hung in the far corner. Fletcher fiddled with the small translation box that was set on the counter, and suddenly Sasa could understand the words that were being said on the screen. It appeared to be some form of Terran news broadcast. He watched as the view on the screen changed, no longer displaying the forms of several Terrans gathered around a large desk.

Visually, it presented the beautiful form of the Xen'wa Queen. She was dyed in the finest patterning of colors, a great wreath of whites and blue giving away to layers of red and greens that ended with a circle of purple, hope, down at the very bottom. Her colors made it clear to Sasa that she was approaching this treaty cautiously, but at the foundation of her actions was a powerful desire for the future of their species. She leaned over a small table that was set out on the landing pad, all the way down on the surface of Thlassia. She dipped one set of her wing talons into a vat of ink, before gracefully spiraling her signature on the treaty document with a delicate motion that didn't have a single one of her ink tipped talons leaving until her sigil was complete. Her feathers fluttered gently in the winds of change on Thlassia.

Beside her, Boer stood, hands clasped behind her, before she took her turn to sign as the flight feather that was threaded down the document's side waved in the breeze. Sasa knew that it would be one of the Queen's own. Fletcher couldn't help but notice how haunted Boer looked, standing there in the wind. He recalled how bright and fresh she had looked during the initial conference call, before everything had happened. Before Thlassia. Now, she stood there, as though she were forged of something different entirely.

A Terran's voice came from the screen.

"The Galactic community is still in shock today with the repercussions of the Xen'wa-Terran treaty, signed yesterday. The sudden Xen'wa departure from the Council will undoubtedly cause even more to question what role it plays in their species' future. In spite of the short war, the Xen'wa have announced that they have entered into a complete military alliance with the Terran Federation." Abruptly, the screen changed, showing several Terrans sitting at a table talking to one another, each decorated in bright and garish colors. Sasa mentally tuned it out, turning back to Fletcher. He had no interest in their interpretations. He had lived through it, been changed by it.

"Shouldn't the Terrarch have been the one to sign?" he asked, cooing his curiosity at Fletcher.

Fletcher just lowered his bottle slightly and let out a deep, single "Ha!"

A few moments later, Sasa saw the screen cut to the Terrarch's seal, a black and white version of the Earth, divided down the middle. On one side, black representing the dirt and white the water, on the other, the black and white with meaning flipped, fully representing the duality of humanity's insanity. At the bottom of the screen, Terran script, something the Sasa had started to learn to help with his role in the new United Fleet, scrolled. Carefully, he worked his way through it.

"The Terrarch sends a message to Humanity."

The three ambassadors were gathered for a final time in the diplomatic chamber. Boer was still dressed in the outfit that she had been wearing moments ago as she had signed the treaty, her cheeks still warm from the constant wind. Stresi had dyed his feathers again, this time a patterning of sharp whites and soft purples. Gwooon floated calmly in his tank, various colors flickering over his form in waves.

Stresi was the first to speak.

"We Xen'wa have a saying. 'The one who brings the wind of the coming storm.'"

He looked deep into Boer's eyes. For the first time, Stresi understood how much of a mirror they were. He saw the same violent, dangerous winds that belonged to his people. Perhaps it had taken him far too long to truly look, blinded as he was by his pride. He decided that he would have to reflect on just how much his actions had contributed to the way everything played out. "I trust your wind will carry us to interesting places."

Stresi ducked his head a final time, then turned to stride out, before pausing at the door.

"Boer," Stresi said, turning just his head back to her. "How does your species do it? Balance such different halves into one whole?"

Boer stood there, thinking about it. At first, Stresi thought she might not answer. But he understood her now. He knew she would. One of her halves would demand it. She stared down at the table as she processed the question, her eyes heavy with thought and emotion. Eventually, one side of her mouth quirked up.

"We were led to it." She gave a weary smile, her eyes flicked up to Stresi. "Above all, we try."

Stresi let out a sound resembling a grunt, before stepping out, leaving Boer alone with Gwooon. Boer looked at the signed treaty a final time, ran her fingers down the edge of the feather where it dipped and weaved through the treaty, fingers tracing the strange path that it took. Resigned, she closed it and slid it into her briefcase, slotting it right next to its unused twin.

"Now that you have completed your task, will you speak with Gwiiin before you go? She will miss you terribly."

Boer looked up at Gwooon from where she had been looking, down into the depths of her briefcase. When he saw her face, he saw that it had been pulled down. Gwooon could feel the grief that the little one radiated.

"I haven't completed my task. In the end, I wasn't able to," she replied simply, turning to Gwooon's tank. A silence hung between them for a moment. "You know, I never answered the question you asked. Why we accepted your offer to host the talks."

Boer wondered what thoughts were going through Gwooon at the moment. As she looked at his form, it was no longer the strange and fear invoking thing from the horror films. She saw the strength of him, the weight that he carried, the depths of his emotions.

"In the end, I think you did."

Their gazes locked for a long moment, peering deeply into each other once more. Gwooon could see something on her face, some expression that spoke of an emotion that he had seen once before. The very first time that the two had met so that she could become accustomed to the translators.

"Gwooon. Why did the Consensus allow the talks to continue? They saw it all. Surely you discussed abandoning us."

He understood what she was asking. How could the Consensus, those bright and hopeful members of his species, continue to allow one such as her to continue? How could they possibly look upon them and not recoil from their nature? Gwooon drifted in his tank. A mixed display of lilac, green, and blue started working its way around his form.

Boer wondered how he would reply. She knew this was the crux of it all, what everything had actually pivoted around. Would it be fear? Would it be power? As Boer gazed deep into those eyes, she hoped she had been right that first time she spoke with him, so many days and lives ago.

"We discussed it nightly," he said ominously. "We haven't debated on a topic that intensely in a very long time. Generations, perhaps."

Boer could feel the accusation in his gaze, could feel all of the thoughts and terrors that had passed between the different members of the Consensus radiate out from him. She thought of the accusations they must have thrown, the travesties that they had dwelled on.

"It was your proffer to the council."

Boer closed her eyes and braced herself on the table with one hand. A single tear slid down her face.

"A dear friend of my daughter once said that our translators were a powerful message." Gwooon's form was slowly becoming more and more lilac as he spoke. "A device that truly connects the stars. That allows everyone to no longer be separated by the vast distances between them. Delivered by a species that could have instead so easily sent destruction, if they so chose. They offered it simply, in peace." He gazed at her solemnly. "A powerful message, don't you think?"

Boer felt the burden that she had been carrying since she had activated ATHENA lift itself off of her. In its place, a great warmth lightened her soul. She reached into her briefcase and pulled out the second diplomatic binder she had brought with her all the way from Earth.

She walked slowly over to the tank. Gwooon stared out at her from his watery constraints. He eyed that binder with all of the weight of the oceans that he carried with him. It was such a small thing, yet he suspected that it held a similar weight. Boer just smiled up at him. He could see that her natural eye was heavy with moisture.

"I have something so very precious that we wish to discuss."

A while later, Boer stood inside the Terrarch's private chambers.

The two were alone, together.

The doctors had laid her out on her medical bed. Next to her stood several terminals, monitoring the Terrarch with their soft beep beep beeps. Boer looked down at the Terrarch's form, so ravaged by the violence of time and the burdens that it had carried. She reached out one hand and gently cradled that frail hand in hers, young and ready. Boer thought it strange that something so small and delicate could contain such great power. She banished the thought from her mind. It was often the smallest of things on which the universe pivoted, single choices that shaped the paths of everyone, such as someone great choosing to come to someone weak and broken in their time of need. As she raised her eyes, she saw the Terrarch's grays staring back at her.

It did not pierce her.

Boer stared back. The two looked all the way down into and through the depths of the other, their wills dancing around each other. Between their gazes, it all passed.

Boer drank her in, enveloped her, consumed her.

The Terrarch unburdened herself fully. She took all of the pain, hope, love, happiness, sorrow, and dreams that she had gathered over her long, long journey, bundled them into a great wave of gravity, and passed them to Boer. It was a thing of power, responsibility. As it wrapped its way around Boer, she felt its burden and its heavy charge. She understood it now and welcomed it.

She would not bend.

She would not break.

She received her message.

Understanding.

EPILOGUE

It was a calm, comforting evening on Thlassia when the final shuttle made its way down to the landing pad. Gathered around its edges were hundreds of Terrans, each dressed in formal attire that gleamed in the fading bronze light of the expiring star. Among them, a single Xen'wa ambassador standing beside his Queen.

When the shuttle finally landed, hissing as the last vestiges of the engines spooled down, as one, they snapped to attention. Slowly, the ramp lowered down to gently rest on the tarmac. Several cameras began broadcasting the scene across Terran space as figures emerged.

The first was Admiral Fletcher, now dressed in a well-fitted black suit that fluttered softly in the thlassian wind. He walked briskly down the ramp, revealing a large black eye-patch covering his right eye. Reaching the bottom, he stepped to the side and clasped his hands stiffly behind his back. Despite the emotions he carried in his remaining eye, he had a soft smile on his face.

Shortly after, the stocky form of representative Auckland followed, dressed in a sharply pressed, immaculate United Fleet uniform. Upon reaching the end, he stepped opposite of Fletcher, and saluted violently.

The two Terrarchs descended slowly, dressed in loose fitting and flowing white, wrapped gently about their forms. The elder was heavily supported by the younger, each of her steps slow and trembling, betraying the extreme labor they took. Carefully, the elder's legs threatening to falter with the strain, they made their way down the ramp. Unlike the others, they did not stop, immediately continuing on their slow, painful journey across the pad. Auckland and Fletcher waited for them to pass, before falling into a slow step behind them.

They worked their way like this, a slow procession aboard the only structure set upon the waves of the world. Across from them, a small boat bobbed in the waters. It was simple in design, a curved portion on the front with a single cushioned bench in its center. It contained no engine. Beneath the water, dozens of metallic rods stretched out into the depths at even spacing.

By the time they had reached the edge of the platform, the planet's star had started to dip low towards the horizon, splashing the bright bronze with tracings of red and gold. The Terrarch twisted in Boer's arms, embracing her.

She clutched Boer close and delivered her final message, a delicate, intimate thing, meant for her alone.

The Terrarch stared up at Boer. Boer returned that same stare back into her eyes. For a moment, Boer was unsure if she could do it. It would be easier not to. To simply hold onto her. They could keep her. They didn't have to let her go. She could continue to bear humanity's burdens.

A soft, gentle smile played across the Terrarch's face. Her stare softened and she gazed deep into Boer's eyes, brushing a single strand of hair from her face, her hand stopping to cradle Boer's head. She whispered something to Boer that she had said once before, a time so long ago when she was as now, a child in pain.

"This too shall pass."

Without a word, Boer's arms fell to her sides.

Two tentacles, each as thick as Boer's bicep and flecked in the faintest tracings of blue, reached up out of the water and offered themselves to the old Terrarch, bracing her as she stepped into the vessel before being gently eased down into the cushions. Beneath the waves, two hundred Thlassians rose to grasp onto the metal rods, gently pushing the vessel onwards through the waves.

Boer and the rest of the Terrans watched silently as their Terrarch was carried off.

When the vessel arrived at its destination, an unmarked spot surrounded by the waters of the world, the Terrarch shrugged out her clothes and with shaking hands, lifted a small device to seal against her face. It consisted of a small glass dome, a breathing apparatus hanging off the bottom. When she found that she didn't have the strength to stand, her legs collapsing beneath her, she was gently cradled and lifted from the vessel, softly eased into the warm waters below. There they left her, adrift above the nursery, staring down at the vivid life so akin to her childhood. As silent tears rolled down her face, every Terran followed their leader, each offering their own sorrow to Thlassia's waters.

She drifted like that, alone yet not, the star slowly drifting its way further and further to the horizon until, at last, the nursery below was cast into shadowed black.

She was so very, very tired now. She couldn't move her arms or legs. Her breaths were coming in deep rattles. Her eyes began to droop. Beneath her, dozens of small lights began to brighten the darkness, bioluminescent love given off by the life below. As she closed her eyes for the final time, she thought to herself that it was as though she were out amongst the stars, unburdened.

The Terrarch sat on the edge of the platform, silently staring out towards where the last few lines of the system's star still clung to the horizon. Her bare feet hung motionlessly in the water. Behind her, a small construct stood silently.

Gwiiin's motionless form floated next to her, resting

calmly in the water, the gentle waves lapping at her body as it bobbed between two worlds. She had taken her father's place among the Consensus, but for the night, she was here just for her friend. Occasionally, one of her jets would blow a small stream of water across the Terrarch's foot as she maintained her position, but the Terrarch paid it no mind.

They rested like that, together, as the light dimmed.

"It was worth it, you know. Everything." Her voice wavered. "It was worth it. Her dream... to finally rest among friends who could accept us for all that we are."

Her voice hung heavy and rippling through the quiet air.

Gwiiin understood.

As the last light began to disappear, Gwiiin spoke.

"That city you spoke about. Sparta. Did any other cities stand alongside them?"

The Terrarch's eyes became hot, her breath hitching in her chest. It took her a moment to find the word.

"Corinth," she said simply.

Gwiiin digested the word.

"Call us that."

A small smile fought against the tears that now flowed freely down the side of the Terrarch's face.

"It would be our Honor."

ACKNOWLEDGEMENT

Wow. So here it is. My first book.

This book came to me as a thing of great violence. It ripped its way through me. I was driving home from work one day after helping my students (yep, that's right, teacher) with their writing when it dawned in my mind in its totality. In a flash of lightning that speared its way through me, I knew it all. The plot, the characters, the setting, the tone, everything. With great violence, it forced its way from me. Over the course of three days, I wrote what would become the first draft of this, 22,000 words. In that time, I did little other than eat, sleep, and write. It consumed me entirely, forced me to write, forced me to continue birthing it into being.

When it was done, I had a moment to marvel at it when it turned its eyes up to me, pleading. It wanted more. Needed it. But its violence was gone. That pleading was not a forceful thing. And so, as an act of love, I nutured it, let it grow and shine. Writing this book has changed me in a profound way. As it came from me, I felt myself changing. The way that I view parts of the world are now fundamentally different, altered.

I feel the desperate need to thank a few of the people that have helped me along the way.

First and foremost, the obligatory 'my parents.' I say that with an edge of humor, but in all seriousness, thank you. Raising me wasn't always an easy thing. Sometimes it was a thing of difficulty. Thank you.

To my grandmother who will never read this, the time spent in your kitchen reading over the books that you had carefully selected for me, all those trips when you took me to the library to get yet another stack, inspired in me a great love for reading. It is a passion that I carry with me to this day and was the bud of what would become the career that I am passionate about.

To Ms. Denise Parker, you did a small thing one day and thrust into my hands a book on banned speeches, influential powerful things that people weren't talking about. This was done to placate the student that finished early, but it inspired a love of language, of its use and manipulation. Thank you.

To my coworkers. You tolerate me. You indulge me. Most importantly, you nuture me. You set forth an environment where I could actually cherish this idea and bring it forth to the page. Thank you. You've done more for me than you realize.

Finally, I would like to thank the twenty two. They know who they are. Your enthusiasm and passions were a fundamental part in validating a dream of mine and giving me the fortitude to chase it. Whether the world accepts the passions that you put forth into it or not, does not matter. Chase your dream. Take your love and let it grow. From the bottom of my heart, thank you. I will always have your back.

Made in the USA
Middletown, DE
06 October 2024